OFF

Season

Book 1 in the Faceoff Series

Thank you blink-182 for inspiring me to rewrite my entire book, all because of one song.

ONE MORE TIME
blink-182

1:07  3:28

Playlist

ONE MORE TIME
blink-182   3:28

Heartbreak Dream
Betty Who   3:49

I Hear the Bells
Mike Doughty   4:19

Peasants
Houses   6:19

Girls Like You
The Naked And Famous   6:04

The Only Exception
Paramore   4:27

The Way I Loved You (Taylor's Version)
Taylor Swift   4:03

Playlist

Pieces of You
nothing,nowhere.   2:49

Time of Our Lives
Hopeland   3:35

Swing, Swing
The All-American Rejects   3:53

Ruin My Life
Zara Larsson   3:10

Hide Away
Daya   3:11

New Romantics
Taylor Swift   3:50

Fall To Pieces
Avril Lavigne   3:29

Social Media

meagz_the_writer

meagz_the_writer96

1

Olivia

This is *bullshit*. Summers are the best for me. A time to get rid of the stress and spend sixteen *glorious* weeks lounging on the beach and sipping *mocktails*.

My family has taken a trip to our beach house in *Cape May* every summer since I was five. My most incredible childhood memories originate from that town. It's where I'm at my happiest. Me, my parents, and my three brothers.

Until now.

My parents and my oldest brother, Eli, wouldn't be driving down with us. This means I'm stuck with Connor and Marcus. I'm overjoyed to be spending time with them. College and school have kept them busy. This will be the first summer without the whole family and it upsets me. It's as if a cloud of despair is hovering in front of the radiant sun. The news has taken away my shine and left a dull shadow.

The only positive is my best friend, Chelsea, will join us this summer. It's been a while since she's visited the beach house with us, and my parents see it as a consolation for flaking on us.

The icy sea air breezes through my open window. I close my eyes and exhale in delight at the familiar scent. *It feels like home.* The bracing breeze washes over my face as we exit the minivan.

The familiar sight of our beach house irradiates my heart as innumerable memories flicker through my mind. I glance at the porch where Connor broke his arm when he was ten. Eli was chasing him after he'd stolen a valuable hockey puck. He forgot about the stairs and plummeted to the ground. It wasn't funny then, but now it's hilarious.

My brothers unload the bags as I rush to the front door. When it's unlocked, I bolt into our home away from home, scrunching my nose at the misty particles of dust floating in the air.

"Thanks for the help, Liv."

Marcus mutters as he hauls my luggage inside.

"No problem at all." I said as I removed the sheets from the furniture.

I cough as I accidentally inhale the tattered dust before opening all the windows, allowing the earthy breeze to pirouette through the home. The ocean is in perfect view of our beach house. I observe the waves playing tag with the shore. They are captivating as they glide like a ballerina.

A presence looms behind me, but I ignore it.

"It's good to be back." Marcus said.

He stands beside me, equally mesmerized by the ocean. The beauty always takes my breath away, no matter how many times we return. The simplicity of this life is enticing. Worries and fears disappear with the waves.

"It's different without everyone."

"We'll make more memories." He reassures me as he places a hand on my shoulder. "Promise you'll take it easy this summer. Allow yourself to rest."

I know he means well, but his words spark annoyance in me. I clench my jaw and squint my eyes, keeping my focus on the ocean, knowing if I looked at him right now, he'd drop dead.

"You agreed you wouldn't bring it up this summer,"

"I know. This is the last time." He turns to me. "I just want your promise you won't push yourself so hard."

The chilly breeze brushes against my heated face, like a gentle touch soothing the frown lines away. My stiffened shoulders drop. *It's summer.* You can't be upset during summer.

"I promise, I'm feeling better already." I said. "The ocean breeze is the best cure."

He gauges my face for signs of dishonesty, eventually nodding.

"Let's have the best summer."

Tiresome grunts infiltrate the silence. We glance toward Connor as he lugs the ample luggage into the room. He drops it with a groan before running the back of his hand across his forehead.

"That was a lot of work." He sighs, leaning against the doorway.

"I told you not to bring so much stuff." Marcus said.

He squats to inspect the baggage.

"Why did you pack a flint?"

We glance at him with knitted brows. He smiles with a sheepish shrug.

"Mom and Dad aren't here. Who knows what dangers we might encounter? Safety first."

Marcus snorts.

I heard the beeping of a horn from outside. My eyes widen as big as my smile.

"That must be Chelsea."

I rush past my brothers onto the porch, stopping at an unknown *Jeep*. This isn't Chelsea's car. The driver exits the vehicle, and my jaw nearly unhinges from its socket. Arrogant blue eyes meet mine. My annoyance wins over my desire to look away.

"You're not Chelsea." I mutter with folded arms.

"Brilliant observation, *Olive*."

I hate when he calls me that.

I think of all the ways of I could murder Marcus.

Why would he invite *him?*

I refrain from stomping off like an angered toddler. I deliver a glare at Marcus as he walks past, and I charge back inside.

"Whatever issues you and Reed have, don't let it ruin our summer," Connor said.

He approaches me with his hands full of luggage. I thought I'd been subtle with my disregard for Reed Adler, but it seems as if my usually unaware younger brother has picked up on our awkward vibes.

I thought my poker face was solid.

"No problem at all."

I don't plan to spend a single second in his presence. Connor seems satisfied by my response and continues dragging his luggage horde up the spiral staircase. I find his struggles humorous, but I can't help but admire his dedication to lug as much as humanly possible. Two stops are out of the question for him.

Wanting to escape to the sanctuary of my bedroom before Reed and my brother return, I grab as much of my luggage as I can.

"Let me help you." Marcus said.

He rushes toward me and hurriedly grabs the bags from my hold.

"I have it." I insist, grinding my teeth in visible frustration.

"You promised." He said.

I silently cursed him and my inability to break a promise. I sigh and gesture for him to take the lead.

"What are you doing?" I asked Reed as he gathered the last of my belongings.

"Pretending to be a gentleman."

He arrogantly winked before following my brother upstairs. I exhale my toxic thoughts and begrudgingly follow them upstairs. My summer plans have already taken a tragic turn.

Reed

I fucked up. There's no denying that. The moment Olivia walked down the porch all the memories of last summer flashed through my mind. The good and the bad. The pleasure and the pain. Last summer was the brightest and darkest time of my life.

I never thought about the reception I'd receive from her, but the hateful seething took me aback. I expected her to be upset with me, but that was next-level hatred.

The atmosphere is icy as we enter her bedroom. Marcus either doesn't pick up on it, or he's ignoring it. I don't have the same luxury.

"We can unpack later," Marcus said. "I'm not wasting another second getting to that beach."

"Chelsea isn't here yet." Olivia said.

"She'll make a fashionably late entrance, like always."

"You go, I'll wait for her and meet you there."

Marcus shrugs and turns to me for an opinion. I raise my hands. *I'm Switzerland.*

"Fine," Marcus said. "We'll meet you there."

I glance at Olivia, but she's already distracted by her phone, impatiently hitting the screen. I trudge behind Marcus into the hallway.

"You're staying in this room." He points at the one across from Olivia's. "I'll see you in ten minutes."

I collapsed on the bed needing a breather. I'd forgotten how hostile Olivia could be. Her sharp words are as deadly as a knife. Both are capable of inflicting wounds, but only one can be removed.

It was naive of me to think that we could simply move on from the events of last summer. Wishful thinking is for fools addicted to disappointment. I screwed up and it's best if I push it under the rug. I can't have Marcus becoming suspicious of my reckless regrets.

It isn't long before I find myself on the beach with Marcus and Connor. The waves were rippling gently. I make myself comfortable on the soft golden sand stretching out my arms and legs like a starfish. The broad smile on my face is evidence of how much I've missed this. The warm sand is the coziest of hugs. I gaze into the aqua abyss and deeply inhale the salty air.

It's good to be back.

Connor bolts for the waves, but Marcus remains tapping away on his phone.

"Please don't tell me Penelope is already nagging you." I groan as I think of Marcus' ball and chain. "We're supposed to be enjoying the summer with random hookups, and you went and got yourself a girl."

I'd started to think he hadn't heard a word I'd said until his corner lip twitched.

"You know, maybe one day you'll find someone, and I'll be nagging you."

I choke on a scoff as if I'd just swallowed a gallon of ocean water.

"If that ever happens, I give you permission to hit me as hard as you can."

He sniggers and extends his hand towards mine. I shake it to solidify our pact before snatching his phone.

"Now, forget about the parole officer and have some fun with your best friend."

He rolls his eyes and glances over my head.

"Looks like the real fun just arrived."

I turn to find a giggling Chelsea and Olivia approaching us. Chelsea raises her hands in the air with a cheer.

"Summer, bitches!"

Her exclamation garners a few looks, especially from disapproving parents with their children. I groan and toss my head. I already have a migraine and she hadn't said more than five words.

"Hello to you too, Reed." She said.

Her face tenses as if she'd sucked a lemon.

"Just when I thought it was going to be a good summer."

"Well, I plan to pretend you don't exist."

"Sounds good to me."

The humid air thickens due to the awkwardness. I close my eyes to protect myself from the blinding rays. *And I'm not talking about the sun.*

"I'm going for a swim."

I squint my eyes with a grin.

"Have fun, *Olive.*" She raises her middle finger as a silent *fuck you.* My eyes follow the pair all the way to the water before I turn to Marcus. "Your sister hates me."

"You're only realizing that now?" He asked. "I don't know what you did to her last summer, but saying your name has practically become a sin to her."

My stomach muscles are tense. *How much had she told Marcus about last summer?* It couldn't have been much - because I'd be dead. I struggle to keep my face as neutral as possible.

"I have no idea." I said.

I hate lying to him, but it's for the best. For everyone. It's best to leave the past in the past.

Olivia

The sand is stuck to every inch of my skin, and I'm overburdened by the aroma of salt, like a cheap perfume. My stomach ached from laughter as a giant wave splashed over Connor, drawing him into the ocean. Every time he gets up, the waves knock him down again. After several humiliating attempts, the ocean seems to take pity on him and allows him to return to shore. He sulks all the way to Marcus and Reed.

"I wish Eli could have come this summer." Chelsea said.

I smile at her. She'd had a crush on my oldest brother for years, but he'd never seen her as anything more than the best friend of his little sister. But Chelsea is relentless. She always yearned for what she couldn't have, and Eli was no exception.

"It's not the same without everyone." I said in agreement.

The ocean breeze wraps around us like a softened towel, embracing us in the warmth. It moves the sea along like an orchestral conductor.

"Let's agree right now," Chelsea said, as she raised an imaginary cup in her hand. "We'll make the most of the summer. We'll embrace the moment and take on new challenges."

I grin at her enticing and motivating speech before raising my imaginary cup above my head.

"To the best summer ever!"

2

Reed

The night was falling. The sun vanished behind the horizon while Marcus and I were by the bonfire. I gaze at the flame that opened skyward, its golden sparks flickering around us.

Every year on the first day of summer, the vacationing and local youth would gather around the beach for an escape from adult supervision. It's infamous for wild moments and scandalous hookups. *This is precisely what I need now.*

I wince as I take a sip of beer. I was too distracted by the flames to notice that the beer had gotten warm.

It was easy to spot the intoxicated people in the crowd. A trio of men wobbles and sways like the currents. They cackled, overpowering the animated chatter around us. I scoff as one loses their balance and drops, eating the sand.

"This was better last year," I said to Marcus, who was typing on his phone. "Not again." I groan.

He hides his phone behind his back and sheepishly grins like a kid who's caught with their hands in the cookie jar.

"Leave it to Penelope to ruin my buzz when she's not even here."

Desperately seeking something cold, I headed to the keg. I feel a burning gaze on the side of my head. Giggling girls are standing a few feet away, looking at me. I turn to them, and they turn away. *How subtle.*

I don't take my gaze away from them as the shorter blonde looks over her shoulder. She blushes once our eyes connect. I wink and her cheeks redden. I chuckle and fill up my cup with more beer.

"Hey."

I knew it was the blonde without looking. I take another sip before spinning to face her. She bites the corner of her lip as she twirls the ends of her locks around her finger. She juts out her hip.

"Hi." I said, as I scoped her from head to toe.

"You're cute."

Direct. I like that.

"Just cute?"

A drawn-out giggle escapes her lips. If she wasn't so attractive, I would have made an excuse to leave.

"What's your name?" She asked, stepping closer to me.

"Reed."

"Even your name is sexy." Her voice is annoying. Like nails on a chalkboard, but she's nice to look at, so I'll let it pass. "I'm Alyssa."

She placed her hand on my biceps and batted her eyelashes as if she expected me to swoon.

"Want to get out of here, Reed?" She asked.

I grin before gulping the rest of my drink.

"I was hoping you'd ask."

I touch her lower back, winking playfully at Marcus. He shakes his head with a chuckle as I walk away with the blonde bombshell.

Olivia

I feel at home in the crowd, as if I'm absorbing everyone's excitement. I feed off the laughter and jubilation. The moon's glow made the languorous tide glitter. The murmuring of the waves is hypnotic, like a siren's call. I gaze into the dark abyss until Chelsea thrusts a cup in front of my face.

I raise it to my nose, wincing at the pungent smell. As if she'd mixed every single type of alcohol in existence. I take a tentative sip and choke on the burning sensation. It's worse than cough syrup.

"I think I added too much alcohol." Chelsea winces after a sip from her cup.

I chuckle.

"Really?" I asked. "I had no idea."

I take the cup from her hand.

"How about we settle for some good old-fashioned beer?" I suggested.

She sighs in relief.

"Please."

I stand to the side, waiting for the keg line to clear. I look around the area in search of Marcus or Connor, but they're both missing. The group of guys dawdles around the keg as they shove each other, howling like wolves. I roll my eyes.

"Excuse me," I said before they directed their focus on me. "Could you move away from the keg? Some of us are trying to use it."

They glance at each other before bursting into laughter as if I'd just delivered the funniest punchline in existence. One falls to the floor and rolls over. The tallest of the group struts towards me, towering over me to look menacing. *I'm not one to be intimidated.* I stand my ground, not breaking our intense eye contact.

"Is there a problem here?" A voice asked.

I turn to glance at the *Dylan O'Brien* lookalike. He raises his brow.

"I don't think that's any of your business." The burly guy approaches him. "She was crying for my attention, and I gave it to her."

My jaw tightens at his vulgar behavior. I reach into my bag.

"Hey, douchebag, this discussion is between me and you."

It's like a scene out of *Jack and the Beanstalk.* He may be the giant, but I'm not Jack.

The moment he's close enough, I draw the taser gun from my bag and lodge it into his side. There are all-around gasps as he collapses to the ground with a groan. I bite my lip to stifle a laugh and the *Dylan O'Brien* guy seems to bite off a grin of his own. I place the weapon back in my bag and step over the guy's curled-up body to pour myself and Chelsea our drinks.

"I've been to a lot of parties in my life, but I've witnessed nothing like that."

I glance at the giant jerk as his friends attempt to haul his heavy body up. I turn my attention to the attractive stranger who came to my aid.

"I have three brothers. The remote was always a source of brutal fights."

He chuckles.

"I was hoping to be the hero so I could impress you, but it doesn't seem you need any saving."

His dazzling smile makes me beam.

"I don't, but I appreciate you trying."

His head drops with a dashing smile.

"Would you like a drink?" I asked.

"Sure." He said and approached the keg beside me.

He glances at both drinks in my hand.

"Are both for you?"

I blush and shake my head.

"One's for my best friend," I said, remembering that Chelsea was still waiting for me. "I should get back to her."

His smile falters. He nods his head.

"I should get back to my friends." He said. "See you around, taser girl."

My cheeks burn from my wide grin. My eyes follow his retreating figure until he's out of my sight.

"What is this? I've heard that you tasered someone?"

My smile drops at the unwanted presence.

"He was being a jerk. He deserved it."

I turn to gaze into Reed's bloodshot eyes. His head moves side to side as if he's balancing a bowling ball.

"Is it wrong that your being feisty turns me on?" He smirks.

I scoff.

"Well, get over it." I seethe. "Those days are over."

His smirk fades.

"Is it because of that guy you were with?"

I furrow my brows. *Where is this coming from?*

"No," I said. "It's because you're nothing but a jerk!"

I resist the urge to bring out the taser again.

"What did I do?"

Either he's drunk or trying to provoke me, because no one can be *this* clueless.

"Did last summer slip your mind?"

He scratches his chin in thought as his eyes glaze over.

"Honestly, I'm too drunk for this conversation."

Typical.

"Whatever, Reed."

I scoffed as I shoved past him. Chelsea's eyes widen as I approach her. She was in deep discussion with two other girls but ran over to me.

"Where have you been?" She asked.

"Sorry," I said with a sheepish smile. "I got preoccupied."

Her brows knit in concern.

"Is everything okay?"

I nod my head, hoping my smile is believable.

"I am now."

She slithers her arm around mine.

"We should enjoy the rest of the night."

I giggle as she drags me back to the girls. Despite Reed and the alpha jerk, tonight was my best summer night yet.

3

Reed

I must have been hit by a bus last night. Or I drank more than I thought. Both are likely. My head feels as if I'd gone three rounds with a professional boxer taking hit after hit. I lift myself from my bed but regret it as a wave of nausea bubbles in my stomach. I rush to the bathroom as fast as my wobbling legs would allow before dumping my contents out. I'm too preoccupied to turn around and look, but I hear laughter coming from behind me.

"Guess the run we planned is canceled."

Marcus.

Without looking at him, I show him the middle finger. His laughter returns. Every chuckle feels as if it's melting my brain.

"By the way, who was the girl I saw sneaking out of the house?"

My brain throbbed from trying to remember anything from last night. A few fragments pop up, but most of it is a hazy blur.

"I think her name was Madison." I said, once my stomach settled.

My arms wobble as I attempt to lift myself from the ground.

"Classy, Reed." Marcus said, before helping me lean against the tub.

The light in the room seems sharper. I place my head in my hands to shield my sensitive eyes.

"You're a mess." Marcus scolds. "Come downstairs when you're ready. Olivia made muffins."

The thought of food made me queasy once more. I take a few deep breaths before mustering the strength to walk downstairs to the kitchen. The greasy smell of grilled bacon wafts through my nostrils. My stomach rumbles.

I slug into the kitchen, unsuspecting of the awkward tension in the air. It's only me and Olivia in the room.

"Hi." I said as I scratched the back of my neck.

My throat is as dry as a desert.

"Hey," she places the muffins out. "Alyssa told me to tell you she'll text you later."

My brows furrow. *Alyssa?* She must have sensed my confusion as she scoffs.

"The girl you hooked up with last night." She said, as if trying to explain *calculus* to a toddler.

"Isn't her name Madison?"

Her eyes bulge out of the sockets.

"Is that supposed to be a joke?" I drew my lower lip between my teeth and shrugged. "Reed, her name is Alyssa. That wasn't even close."

"How can you be certain?"

She tosses her hands up into the air before dropping them at her side.

"She introduced herself to me twenty minutes ago."

I raise my brows before reaching over the counter for a strip of bacon. Her eyes bore into me, but I ignored it. She scoffs and turns back to stacking the multitude of muffins. Neither of us spoke, suffocating in the sudden thick air. My eyes dart everywhere but in her direction.

My lungs open the moment Marcus enters the room. As if his entrance popped the bubble of awkwardness.

"Has anyone seen Connor?" Marcus asked.

"He texted me he was staying over with some friends he met last summer." Olivia said.

I don't know if he was oblivious to the tension in the air, or if he's got a phenomenal poker face. I remained under the radar and ate my breakfast.

Olivia may sometimes be a cold bitch, but she knows how to cook.

"Who is ready for a beach day?"

Chelsea's irksome voice infiltrates the silence. She's a notorious partier, but in my eyes, she's always been a notorious nuisance. I purse my lips as she steals the last strip of bacon. The grease cured my hangover, but her presence has made me queasy all over again. I push myself away from the counter.

"I'm ready to go when you are." I said to Marcus as I breezed past him, feeling a wave of annoyance wash over me.

The sun was like a lover's kiss on my cheek. As we waddle along the sand looking for the perfect place to set up our stuff. Despite the enormous crowd, we found a spot on the beach. I laid my towel out on the sand before stretching my arms above my head.

I scope the surroundings as everyone seems to have the time of their lives. Something we should be doing.

I noticed a group of girls a few feet away, one of whom I recognize. *Alyssa.* That's if Olivia wasn't lying to me about her name. I reached for the football I packed and tossed it toward Marcus. He caught it.

"Why would you do that?" He asked.

I tilt my head toward the girls. His eyes follow before realization sets in.

"What's the plan?"

He sighed, knowing he had no choice. *He does, but he knows I'd do this for him.*

"Toss it in their direction."

I bolt towards the group. We've done this play so many times over the summers that I could do it blindfolded. It's my most successful play. I jump in the air and capture the ball with both hands. They squeal as I land in the circle with a thud. I resist the urge to smirk as they flock around me like curious vultures. They fawn over me, scoping me for any visible bruises. I repress a smirk.

"Are you okay?" The strawberry blonde-haired girl asked.

"I'm good," I lift myself from the sand. "Are you all okay?"

I couldn't help but find it humorous how easily they were concerned by my fake fall. Either they're naïve, or I have a career in Hollywood waiting for me. It's a win-win for me either way. The strawberry-blonde girl approached me as the light made the freckles on the apples of her cheeks more prominent.

"I know it was all fake. Good attempt though."

I gulp. Perhaps these girls aren't as naïve as I thought.

"I have no idea what you're talking about."

It's best to feign innocence. She might be bluffing. No one has ever seen past my tricks before.

"It's the oldest trick in the book."

She scoffed, but the smug grin on her face made me think she was impressed.

"It's also the most effective."

I folded my arms across my chest and dropped my left eye in a wink.

"It depends on who you're using it on because it's not working on me."

I can't help but chuckle.

"It got you over here talking to me. Seems like it worked just fine."

Her smug grin drops. I got her like a fish on a hook.

"Well played." She said. "I'm Brynlee."

"Reed."

Her friends join us, and I spot the familiar face. It's the girl from this morning. Her name slipped from my mind, but I can remember the annoying hair twirling. I can't believe I found it attractive twenty-four hours ago and now it's annoying. I should have known better. However, I couldn't have known that I would like a girl, only to have hooked up with her friend the night before. Only an idiot could have gotten themselves into this situation.

Typical me.

"Hey."

I'm trying not to make it obvious that I cannot remember her name. I'm not sure if I've been successful or if she's too vapid to notice.

"I was wondering when I was going to see you again."

I cast my eyes in every direction but hers, scratching the back of my neck and biting the corner of my lip.

"I better get going." I look around for Marcus, only to find him in the water with Connor, Olivia, and Chelsea. "My friends are waiting."

She pouts, expecting me to drop everything to help her feel better. I wave before bolting off. *I couldn't have gotten out of that situation any quicker.*

Olivia

The ocean water has become my second scent. I spent so long being enveloped in the methodic waves with Chelsea that my fingers started turning to shriveled prunes. Marcus and Connor opted to remain swimming while we made our way to our towels.

"I'm starving."

I wring the water out of my hair.

"Ice cream sounds like a good idea." Chelsea said.

We burst into laughter as my stomach grumbles the moment she mentions ice cream. We skip along the sand until we reach the ice cream truck. Chelsea glances at the options on the menu above the middle-aged man's head. I don't bother looking, knowing I'm going to get the same flavor I do every time.

Mint chocolate chip.

"Taser girl."

My stomach flutters at the semi-familiar voice, and I turn to find my mystery guy grinning at me with his hands tucked into the pockets of his swimming trunks. I cringe as I smile at him as if he's a celebrity and I'm waiting for an autograph. I shake my *fangirl* thoughts away and clear my throat.

"Mystery guy."

He chuckles and glides his fingers through his sun-kissed locks. The sun reflecting against his glimmering eyes reminds me of melting caramel. I couldn't look away.

"It's Wyatt." He said. "Wyatt St. James."

He extends his hand out in a formal greeting. I place my hand in his, shivering as his warm skin heats my cooled-down body.

"Olivia Huxley."

His radiant smile widens.

"I'd been kicking myself the entire night and morning for never having asked your name." He said. "I was hoping fate would give me a second chance."

My cheeks burn hotter than the scorching sun.

"It seems fate has been on your side."

He does not hide his provocative gaze as his eyes flicker up and down my body.

"I couldn't be more grateful." He said. "The moment I saw you, I needed to know more about you."

"What if I'm boring, and that dreaming was for nothing?"

"You seem to forget I witnessed you attacking someone with a taser." His brows furrow. "You don't have a boring bone in your body."

I glanced behind him to find a guitar case strapped to his left shoulder. How did I miss that?

"You play the guitar."

"I do."

This time, he's the one blushing. He kicks at the sand as his ears burn. He's holding back a grin, making his dimples more prominent.

"That's cool," I said to comfort his distressed demeanor. "I always wished I could learn."

His head perks up.

"I could teach you sometime."

I wanted to seize the opportunity right away, but I didn't want to come across as too eager and intimidate him. I bit my bottom lip to suppress my smile and nod my head.

"Sure." I said, attempting to seem nonchalant.

He scratches his biceps as he seems to debate something.

"My band is playing tonight on the beach if you want to watch us perform?"

He seems so vulnerable, as if my saying *no* would shatter him into microscopic pieces. I couldn't help but think how his being in a band has made him even more attractive.

I've always been a sucker for musicians.

"I'd love to watch you perform." I cringe at my eagerness. "You and your band, I mean."

He grins.

"I will dedicate a song to you."

I'd melted from his words. Who doesn't want someone to dedicate a song to them? It's been my dream forever, my secret wish.

No matter how hard I tried, I couldn't contain my giddiness. His dazzling smile has a kaleidoscope of butterflies swarming around my stomach. I couldn't get enough of it, like an adrenaline rush.

"I'd love that."

He brushes his fingers through his locks. Even his hair is gorgeous.

"I didn't think I could have been more excited for tonight, but you've made it even more special."

My cheeks became flushed. Ruby red.

"I'll see you tonight."

"I'm counting down the hours."

I'd been on cloud nine since my conversation with Wyatt. The moment I'd rejoined Chelsea, I filled her in on all the sordid details. If you could even describe it as sordid. I'd waited for tonight and it arrived. As tragic as it may be, it's the most excitement I've had in over a year.

The partiers on the beach are as lively as the ocean waves, swaying back and forth along with the music. I feed off their excitement as the melody flutters against my eardrums, vibrating with jubilation.

Chelsea approaches with two red cups in her hand. She offers me one with a wide grin.

"Cheers to us!" she said. I tap my cup against hers in a silent cheer. "And cheers to a potential summer romance."

My ears burn. I think she's even happier about Wyatt than I am. My last summer romance crashed and burned, and the ashes got blown away by the harsh winds. Fading into oblivion.

I push my mistakes to the back of my mind. It's time to focus on the present.

"Hello, Olive."

I wince at the dreaded nickname. Leave it to *him* to penetrate my bubble of happiness.

"What are you doing here?" Chelsea asked Marcus and Reed.

"We met a group of girls this morning and they invited us." Reed said.

"Correction, *he* met a group of girls," Marcus interjected. "I'm just here to play *wingman*."

I scrunch my nose in disgust. Reed's usual crude behavior doesn't shock me anymore. He tends to stray from woman to woman.

Chelsea nudges me out of my judgmental thoughts and tilts her head to the right. My eyes follow. I grin as Wyatt stands with his group of friends, but his eyes are already on me. My stomach flutters as he excuses himself from his friends to approach me. I met him halfway.

"I'm so glad you're here." He said.

I freeze as he wraps his arms around me. His heavenly scent tickles my nostrils. His embrace is like a surprise gift on *Christmas*. You didn't know you wanted it until you got it.

"I couldn't miss a performance from the next biggest band."

I could have sworn I saw him blush.

"You haven't even heard me perform."

"I know I'll be impressed."

An infuriating voice cuts our playful banter short.

"What the *fuck* are you doing here, *St. James?*"

Our heads whip as Marcus and Reed approaches us. Reed's clenched jaw makes the veins in his neck more visible. I don't think I've ever seen him so angry.

"I could ask you the same thing, Adler."

My brows knit in confusion at the unexpected interaction.

How do they know each other?

Even Marcus seems tense.

My eyes dart back and forth between the *alpha male* stand-off. However, it's between Reed and Wyatt. I chalked it down to my brother not being one for confrontation, while Reed fed off it. He thrives in conflict.

Marcus steps toward Reed and leans down to his ear.

"Let it go. We came here to enjoy some music, not pick a fight."

His words did nothing to ease Reed's anger. I'm almost certain his anger amplified.

"Good to know you came to watch me play."

His smug grin is a contrast to the usual friendly face I've seen during our brief interactions. Reed steps forward before he's blocked by Marcus' outstretched arm.

"Let's go get something to drink."

He'd always been the peacemaker. If he could avoid conflict, he'd jump through hoops to do it. The wheels in Reed's mind worked overtime as he glared at Wyatt before relenting to my brother's suggestion. They stalk off, leaving me rocking on the soles of my feet.

Wyatt locks eyes with me. The anger on his face fades away.

"How do you know them?" He asked.

"Marcus is my brother."

He breathes through his teeth.

"This just got awkward."

"How do you know them?"

"We have quite the history." he said as he scratched the back of his neck. "Your typical sports rivalry."

My eyebrows furrow.

"You play hockey?"

It's the only sport my brother and Reed play. I could only surmise he does, too.

"My entire life."

I scratch my arm as I consider how outrageous the entire situation is. The first guy I've liked in over a year has a hostile history with my brother. The irony is that he's not the worst dating option.

It seems I've already decided.

"Well, whatever issues you have, has nothing to do with me."

He smiles at my answer.

"I'm glad you said that."

I was about to reply when a group of guys called his name, motioning for him to join them.

"I better get ready."

"Good luck." I smile.

"With you here, I already have luck." He said before rushing off to join his friends.

With a scorching face, I saunter toward Chelsea as she waits.

"Is it just me or has drama seemed to follow you a lot more lately?" She asked.

"I was just thinking the same thing."

I exhale in frustration. We listen to the bands that are brave enough to stand on stage and I fall in love with their melodies, but my mind is only focusing on hearing Wyatt's band perform. The anticipation has been eating away at me like a hungry vulture.

They walk up on the stage, soaking in the crowd's excitement. Despite three other guys being in his band, he's the only one I locked my eyes on. I'm enthralled by the way he bewitched me with the melody echoing from his bass guitar as if he was serenading me. The roaring applause snaps me out of my daydream as his band waves at the adoring crowd before exiting the stage. My heart skips a beat as he brushes past the crowd. I choke on a gasp as he stands in front of me. He takes deep breaths, as if recovering from the surge of adrenaline. His sweaty locks stuck to his forehead, but he still looked insanely attractive.

"Hey." He said through bated breath.

"Hey," I wince at my uncharacteristic introversion. "You were great."

He exhales as if he'd been holding his breath this entire time.

"I'm so happy to hear that." He said. "I was afraid you'd hate it."

"That was never a possibility."

He brushes his fingers through his hair and glances at his feet. I spotted his rosy cheeks.

"Would you like to take a walk with me?" He asked. "We could get to know each other more."

The corners of my lips rise.

"I would love to."

We trail through the sand, side by side. The smile on my face never falters. *Perhaps I'll have my summer romance after all.*

4

Reed

I hate Wyatt St. James. I've hated him since
the day I met him in my sophomore year of
high school. As if we were destined for rivalry.
Everything about him rubbed me the wrong
way. He's a natural dickhead.

Now I'm forced to share a beach with him.

He's also sunken his teeth into Olivia like a
blood-thirsty leech. Another name to tick off his
notorious *hookup list.*

He makes me look like a saint.

I trudge downstairs, rubbing my eyes until I
see stars. I follow the faint voices into the

kitchen. Marcus is leaning against the counter with his phone attached to his ear.

"I miss you too." He said.

I roll my eyes. There's only one person he could be talking to.

Penelope.

I turn around, not in the mood for their insufferable declarations of love, and waltz into the living room at the same moment Olivia enters through the front door. I fold my arms across my chest like a concerned parent having waited up to reprimand their child for missing curfew.

"Where have you been, young lady?" I asked.

I chew my bottom lip to hold a smile back. She rolls her eyes in reply before moving toward the staircase. I block her. I raise my brow, not giving up my facade.

"I'm tired, Reed." She sighs. "I'm not in the mood for your games."

All playfulness drains from my body.

"You were with that jackass, weren't you?"

Her brows furrow.

"Why is that any of your business?"

"I'll take that as a yes."

"Again, why is it your business?"

Her voice is laced with disdain.

"I was just asking," I said and raised my hands in surrender. "You've been gone the entire night."

"We were just talking."

I scoff.

"Wyatt St. James doesn't *just* talk."

She rubs her brow as her shoulders sink. A lock of hair falls in front of her eyes, but she doesn't move it away.

"I'm too exhausted for this."

She storms past me, intentionally colliding her shoulder with mine. I grunt at her unexpected strength. I rubbed the injured spot.

It's like playing hockey.

With a hefty sigh, I returned to the kitchen, pleased that Marcus had ended his sappy call with Penelope.

"What are you going to do about the situation with your sister?"

He takes a sip of water and shrugs.

"There's nothing I can do." He said. "She makes her own decisions."

I scoff.

"So, you're going to let her be another one of his conquests?"

I folded my arms across my chest.

"What else am I supposed to do?" He asked in defeat. "If I tell her not to see him, she'll do the opposite."

I mull his words over, knowing he's right. She'd always been rebellious and independent. She detests being told what to do.

"He's trouble."

He nods his head in agreement.

"I know." He said. "We have to be vigilant about her."

❧

The sun's rays cast down on the beach with brute intensity. There is limited shade for such a hot day. I'd gone back and forth from the ocean to the shore. However, the moment I stepped onto the sand, the sun had already dried my body off.

Chelsea's enormous umbrella could provide me with some shade to cool off, but I would have to tolerate that jerkoff.

I'd rather melt in the sun.

I'm soon joined by Connor, who takes a seat next to me, just out of touching distance of the waves. He offers me a can of *Monster,* which I happily accept. As we observe the people in the ocean, we don't speak and watch as a few of them get pummeled by an unsuspecting wave.

"What's the deal with you and this Wyatt guy?" He asked.

My laughter dies down, which is not unexpected. Connor has never been subtle. Whatever goes on in his head, he voices out loud.

"I never liked him," I said with a shrug. "He's not a good guy."

Connor snorts.

"There must be a better reason."

I raise my brow at him.

"What are you saying?"

"Think about it, Reed." He said, turning his body to look at me with raised brows. "It's not like we're the greatest either."

I recoil from his words as if he'd just slapped me in the face.

"Neither of us is boyfriend material." He said. "We can't all be like Marcus."

I glance over my shoulder toward my best friend as he laughs at something his sister said. My shoulders drop.

Marcus has always been your perfectly well-rounded *boy next door*. He had everything figured out.

An unattainable task for me.

It's one of the many reasons we became best friends. Despite our thirteen-year friendship, I remain the same mess, wishing his good nature would rub off on me.

"You don't know Wyatt as I do."

We fall into silence once again, everything around us becoming background noise.

Olivia

My mother would always take us out for ice cream in this weather. We'd go to *Joey's* ice cream shop and have three scoops each. It's always been my fondest memories of my summers here.

Now she isn't even here.

My parents have been acting strange for a while. I was hoping it was just my imagination, but after they broke the news that they wouldn't join us for summer, it became clear.

I can't help but think I'm to blame.

Last year was a challenge for everyone. The trauma is still shadowing us. Lingering like a putrid stench.

I gaze out my bedroom window as the sun disappears behind the horizon. It looks as if the ocean is swallowing it.

"What are you looking at?" Marcus asked as he leaned against my doorway.

"The sun."

"What's on your mind?"

The corner of my lip twitches. He knows me so well.

I debated in my mind whether to make up a story or come clean.

He'd always understand. My gut chants into my ear.

"Do you know why Mom and Dad passed on joining us?"

I want to tear the band-aid off. His footsteps echo through the room before his presence looms beside me.

"What are you talking about?"

His tone isn't accusing, just confused.

"It's because of me." I bit my lip to hold back a river of tears. "Last year was torture for everyone."

He places his arms on my shoulders, forcing me to look at him. He crouches down until we're at eye level.

"Listen to me." His voice is stern. "What happened was not your fault. You didn't ask for it. Nothing that is going on is *any* fault of yours."

"So, you admit it," I said through sniffles. "Something is going on."

I've been drowning in these thoughts ever since we arrived. I'd reach the surface and momentarily catch my breath before the menacing thoughts flooded me again.

It's a vicious cycle.

The back of my eyes burns as the tears make my vision blurry. I could only hold them back for so long before they overpowered me. Marcus rushed to my side and wrapped his arms around me in a comforting embrace. My tears stain his shirt, but it doesn't seem to faze him.

"I honestly don't know what's going on." He said. "I can sense it too, but I know it has nothing to do with you."

I inhaled, feeling as if his words helped lift the boulder of burden off my shoulders. I would always have him by my side.

"Thank you."

He smiles and playfully punches my shoulder.

"Let's get some ice cream before the bonfire."

I couldn't hold back my grin. I can never turn down ice cream.

Every *Cape May* night is a party. No exceptions. The beach has no solitude. It's disrupted during the day, followed by nightly chaos. Teenagers invaded the land in hopes of getting a few hours away from their overburdening guardians. It brings a sense of freedom even if it's only temporary.

Freedom is overrated.

I used to want to escape my parents and hang out with friends in the summer, but now I would do anything to have another summer moment with them. I wish they tagged along.

Arms around my waist make me squeal as Chelsea tackles me onto the sand. I groan at the unexpected force. Her giggles flutter with the wind.

"Why did you do that?"

I sit upright and direct my icy glare at her. She shrugs.

"I thought it would be funny." She said. "Let's go get a drink."

I follow her through the standard overbearing crowd and to the large keg. It seems to be filled to the brim with ice-cold ale. I pour my drink, hoping to distract myself from darting my eyes all over in search of Wyatt.

I planned to play it cool and not look too eager to see him, but once my eyes locked with him a few feet away, I nearly dropped my cup.

"Olive!"

The annoying voice of Reed exclaimed as he approached. He brushed past Chelsea and towards the keg and filled his cup to the brim before chugging all the contents. He sighs and catches his breath.

"Are you in a rush or something?" Chelsea snipes.

He shrugs and refills the cup. He takes a smaller sip this time.

"I've got friends to meet up with." he said, followed by a wide smirk. "Female friends."

I scoff and fold my arms across my chest.

"You're disgusting."

"I love it when you talk dirty to me." He drops his left eye in a wink.

I purse my lips. How can someone be so infuriating?

"Let's go, Chels."

"Leaving so soon?"

The smug look on his face makes it obvious he's trying to get a reaction out of me.

"We have somewhere to be."

"Then I guess we can gossip some other time." He takes another sip of beer. "Have a lovely evening."

I glare at his retreating figure before returning my attention to Chelsea - but she's already gone.

My heart palpitates as Wyatt approaches me with a sheepish grin.

"Hey." He said. I couldn't help but admire how adorable his crimson cheeks were as he scratched the back of his neck. He bounces on the balls of his feet. "Do you want to take a walk with me?"

"I'd love to."

We stroll in silence as the sea softly douses the shore, creeping steadily towards us. However, the calming waves do nothing to soothe my rattling heart. I hold back a grin as our hands brush, wanting to hold his hand, but I lack the confidence. I'm as cowardly as the lion in *The Wizard of Oz*.

"So, are you in college?" I asked, hoping to strike up a conversation.

"I am." He said. "Starting my sophomore year after the summer."

Just like Marcus.

"Are you enjoying it?"

"It has its perks." He grinned. "What about you? Are you in college?"

I nod my head.

"My freshman year officially begins after the summer."

I tuck my hands in my pockets.

"Have you decided on a school?"

"Ohio State."

"The same as your brother." He said, but I couldn't help but notice his slight grimace.

"I didn't choose it because of my brother," I said. "He went there because of me."

"What do you mean?"

I deeply inhale the salty air. The ocean waves became the background noise to my ruthless thoughts.

Why did I say that?

"It's a long story."

In theory, I could have summed it up in a few sentences, but it's not something I'm willing to share. I'm hoping to leave the past in the past. The soothing waves are a contrast to my brutal thoughts as the faulty memories flickered through my mind like a fast-paced *Instagram* reel.

Every day is a struggle to keep them dormant. The tragedies keep escaping like prisoners, waiting for the moment of vulnerability to attack.

"Those are always the best." His voice brings me back to Earth. "When you're ready, I'll be here to listen."

My stomach bubbles with appreciation. I'd expected him to insist I tell him, but he respected my decision of secrecy. It may seem like the bare minimum, but few people respect privacy anymore - it's admirable.

5

Reed

I woke up drenched in salt water. I shot up with a gasp as the unexpected sub-zero temperature chilled me to the core. I wiped the water from my eyes to find Marcus standing above me with a tipped bucket.

"Why would you do that?" I asked.

My throat burned as I spoke. It's as dry as the *Atacama Desert.*

"You passed out on the beach."

I furrow my brows, finally noticing the sand beneath me. The moon is glimmering along the waves. The party is lifeless.

"Where did everyone go?"

I clutch at my throbbing head.

"The party ended two hours ago." He said. "I've been looking everywhere for you."

My stomach feels queasy, but not from the excessive amount of alcohol I've consumed. Marcus' judgmental look resembles a disappointed parent. A simple gaze from him makes you question all your life choices.

"You found me."

I lifted myself from the sand. I lose my balance, but Marcus' swift reflexes save me from falling face-first.

"I thought we were done with this."

"The getting drunk part, or you having to look for me hours later?" I asked with a smirk.

"Both."

I squint my eyes as I gaze into the darkened sky, completely awestruck by the sight of two moons.

I underestimated how much I drank.

"I'm sorry."

He wraps my arm around his shoulder as he takes on most of my weight. It's become a tradition for us. I drink myself into a stupor and he carries my inebriated self home.

The perfect friendship.

"You're going to be really sorry tomorrow morning." He chuckles.

The entire situation is hazy as if I'm a spectator to the spectacle. I'm physically present, but my mind is in another reality.

I don't remember the trip back to the beach house until I fell face-first onto my silk sheets. Marcus turns me onto my side, and I groan at the queasy knots forming in my stomach.

"You better not throw up on me."

I only manage a whine. His distant laughter fades as my fluttering eyes lose their battle to sleep.

I clutch at my throbbing head, wincing at the déjà vu. It's as if my brain inflated like a balloon before exploding.

You'd think I'd have learned my lesson.

I reached for my phone. I slept through the morning.

An abundance of texts from Alyssa flooded my screen. I scrolled through a few before locking my phone and tossing it to the end of my bed. I fall onto the plush pillows and place my arm over my eyes.

"Glad to see you're alive."

Marcus bursts through the door.

"It doesn't feel like it."

My stomach churns. I sink further into my silk sheets and place a hand on my burning forehead.

"Let's go to *Josie's.*"

Despite the agonizing migraine, my stomach grumbled at the thought of a three-stack pancake.

The perfect hangover cure.

Josie's is the local diner we would frequent every hangover morning. It's a tradition we've had for ages - ever since the moment we first sneaked some alcohol during a party Marcus' parents were hosting. Curiosity drove our young, reckless selves to explore the hype.

We instantly regretted it once we woke up the next morning, fearing an imminent death. It didn't take Marcus' dad long to figure out what we'd done, and he gave us an earful. Afterward, his oldest brother, Eli, brought us to Josie's - introducing us to our hangover tradition.

Lately, it's become more of me suffering a hangover and Marcus taking care of me as if I am a petulant child.

Josie's is walking distance from the beach house, but when you're hungover, it feels hours away. The morning sun shone down with a vengeance, frying my eyes like an egg.

"How many times do I need to lecture you about drinking so much?" Marcus asked.

We make ourselves comfortable in our favorite corner booth. It has the perfect view of the town area through the large window. It's close enough to the beach that you can still smell the delightful salty air.

"There used to be a time when you'd have been as hungover as me."

He chuckled.

"True," he said. "One of us needed to grow up."

I smirk despite the thumping in my head. He's only a few months older, but it's as if he matured years overnight.

"Or it's because Penelope's dullness rubbed off on you." I said.

He took it in good spirits and playfully punched my shoulder.

"Come back to me when you've fallen in love." He said. "If the day ever comes."

His words irked me, and I do not know why. It might be the unshakeable guilt I feel every time the topic arises.

The fact that I was once in love is something I can never share with my best friend, and it bothers me. He can't know I would have risked anything for someone in the past.

He could never know that the very person was his sister.

I lean against the table, hoping to be as stoic as possible. I avoid eye contact for fear he might sense my discomfort. He's always been good at gauging my mood.

"You'll be the first to know if that day comes."

I'm drowning in lies.

I'll drown in my deception if I paddle for too long.

Olivia

Spending time at the golf club was the best part of my summer. The first time my parents ever brought me here, I was hooked.

It holds an abundance of memories. My mom and I would spend every Saturday bonding while my dad took my brothers to play golf. She'd order a mocktail for me and I'd momentarily feel like a grownup. I remember the disappointment on her face when I'd showed an interest in golf instead of our weekly *gossip sessions.*

What I would do to have my entire family here.

"When you said you had something fun planned, golf was the last thing on my mind." Chelsea said as she approached me.

She pushes her sunglasses down to peer over the lens. She scrunches her face at the expanse of green land. I resist the urge to roll my eyes at her blatant dislike for anything active.

A pair of golf carts pull up beside us. Connor and Marcus are in one. Marcus is behind the wheel. Reed has the other.

"Who gave you guys golf carts?" Chelsea asked.

"We stole them." Reed said.

His tone is relaxed, and you'd think he's kidding, but the wide smirk on his face raises suspicion.

"Let's go already." Connor said.

He's always been impatient.

Reed glances at us and tauntingly taps the open space beside him.

"Which of you are ready for the ride of your life?" He asked. "I've been told I'm pretty good, in more ways than one."

I can't help but roll my eyes at his innuendo. His words reek of smugness, but I don't want to engage in an argument and ruin a fun day. However, I couldn't help but burn with rage as he looked at me whilst he spoke.

As if to say:

You know what I'm talking about.

I scoff but suck it up and slide into the seat next to him.

Before I could chastise him for not killing us with his lack of driving skills, he sent the cart surging forward.

Chelsea and I squeal as his laughter booms. He drives with Marcus as if it's the final lap of a *Formula One* race. He swerves and weaves, attempting to block an overtake from Marcus.

The carts nearly collided.

We make it to the first hole with no physical damage.

I don't waste time getting ready to play. I've been waiting for this moment. It's been a while since I've been able to play golf with my brothers. They had the advantage in hockey, but I excel in this sport. I'm ready to crush them. I lined up with a perfect shot, but Reed stood behind me, breaking my concentration.

"Do you need help?" He asked. "I could wrap my arms around you and show you how it's done."

I try not to let his words get to me. I regained my concentration and take the perfect shot, glancing over my shoulder with a satisfied smirk.

"I'm pretty sure I know how it's done."

He bites his bottom lip.

"Maybe you could wrap your arms around me?" He grins. "Show me how it's done."

I know he's trying to rile me up, and no matter how much I command my brain to ignore him. It's working. My body is fuming.

Connor lines up for a shot before completely missing the ball. We burst into a fit of laughter as he places his hand over his eyes in search of the motionless ball. He glances at his feet, his face burning red at the unmoving ball. Marcus steps in, pushes him aside, and sends the ball forward like a pro.

"Show off." Connor mutters from beside me.

I chuckle at his attitude. Connor has always been the light in our familial darkness. He had a knack for brightening the mood and easing the weight of burdens. He's our rock.

After a few hours of outrageous smack talk and one-upping, we called it a day and got some food. I think the bitter back and forth was due to us being *hangry*. My stomach grumbled at the thought of a large bowl of *mac and cheese.*

My comfort meal.

The moment we step into the closest cafe - the familiarity lands a sucker punch on my jaw. All the memories hit me like skilled jabs.

This was always mine and my mom's special place. It feels like eons ago that we'd been here gossiping over a plate of finger sandwiches. It amazes me how quickly tradition can fade into oblivion. How something cherished can become meaningless in the blink of an eye.

Chelsea nudges me with her elbow. Our eyes meet and we telepathically communicate, a skill we have mastered.

Are you okay?

I nod my head as we take a seat beside each other. Everyone grabbed a menu, but I knew exactly what I wanted. *One thick chocolate shake and a bowl of mac and cheese.* My usual.

"You have got to be kidding me." Reed's voice captures our attention.

He's glaring at something behind us. I turn around and bite my lip to hold in a laugh as the waitress approaches us.

"Hey, Reed." She greets him as if he's the only one at the table.

"Hey."

His eyes focus on the menu in front of him as the frosty awkwardness raises goosebumps. He clears his throat. She shakes her head as she returns to reality.

"What can I get you?"

I glance at her name tag. *Alyssa.* The girl whose name Reed repeatedly seems to forget. She pulls a notepad from her apron and clicks her pen. She glances at him with raised brows. I kick Reed under the table. He jumps and directs his angered gaze at me.

Marcus steps in and orders his usual, saving Reed from the insufferable silence. Once she'd taken all our orders and stepped out of earshot. We all burst into a fit of giggles at Reed's uncharacteristic awkwardness. I couldn't help but take sadistic pleasure in his suffering.

"So," Connor said, as he leans over the table as if he's about to share confidential information with us. "I made some friends yesterday, and they invited me to a party tonight. Who is in?"

We happily agreed, vowing this would be a summer of fun and never-ending parties. No one is backing out.

6

Reed

Does everyone have houses this big? As if it would be a disgrace to the neighborhood to have a house with less than twelve bedrooms. Anything less, you're living in poverty.

Who even needs that much space?

There's nothing I hate more than a bunch of pretentious jackasses thinking they're better than everyone because of their wealth.

The rich and the famous always get preferential passes to be assholes.

I glance at the abundance of alcohol littering the kitchen counter. They may be assholes, but they have good taste in booze. I don't know what to choose or where to start.

"You can never go wrong with vodka."

It's as if this person could read my mind.

Brynlee slides alongside me and reaches for the unopened bottle. I smile as her familiar face lightens my spirits.

Maybe this party won't suck after all.

"I trust your judgment."

She'd already poured us two shots each before I could get a word out. I reach for the first one. We clink our glasses together before turning our heads back for the large gulp. I scrunch my face as the bitter water burns my esophagus all the way to my stomach. I cough and she follows suit.

"Think you're brave enough for another one?" She asked with a challenging grin.

"I'm insulted you'd even ask."

We perform the traditional *cheers* before downing the second shot. It tasted even worse than the first. I shake my head and suck in air through my teeth. Despite the putrid taste, I feel more at ease. I'm not sure if it's because of the liquid courage, or Brynlee's calming presence.

"That should get the night going."

She's flawless.

I couldn't help the inappropriate thoughts of her that flitted through my mind. I couldn't help but undress her with my eyes, as she's one of the most attractive women I have ever laid my eyes on.

To avoid further straining in my pants, I look over the crowd on the makeshift dance floor. The sweaty, drunken teens coiled together and jumped to the thumping base of an unfamiliar song.

I walk closer against the counter to hide the obvious tent underneath my tattered jeans, but it deflates the second I spot Olivia standing against the wall with a beer in her hand - with Wyatt St. James hovering over her. He leans down to whisper something in her ear, and she giggles before pushing his chest.

Instant boner killer.

In all the time I've known Wyatt, I don't remember him being funny. He's as dry as a cardboard box.

"Glare any harder, and that guy might just combust." Brynlee's voice brings me out of my twisted thoughts.

"A guy can dream." I don't take my eyes off the pair.

"Is it because you're not a fan of his? Or are you a huge fan of hers?"

"Both."

I clear my throat and square my shoulders.

"She's my best friend's sister. I have to look out for her."

She raises her brows and I can't blame her apprehension. I couldn't convince myself. I watch as she reaches for the bottle of vodka and pours another hefty shot, filling it to the brim. She extends it to me.

"I think you need this right now."

I don't waver in knocking it back, not even wincing this time. My anger masked the bitterness.

"So, care to explain the situation?"

I bit my lip. I split my mind in half - one side is telling me to spill the beans, and the other is telling me not to trust someone I've only known for a few days. However, I've been keeping this secret locked inside for so long. It's time to blow off the dust and bring it out of captivity.

"We dated over the summer."

"I figured as much." She motions for me to get to the point.

"We kept it a secret from Marcus," I said. "We were happy until I screwed it up like I do everything."

She tilts her head.

"What did you do?"

Her intense gaze makes me feel at ease talking to her about this. She isn't seeking gossip, she's curious and concerned.

Could I tell her the truth and trust her to keep it a secret?

I had sealed the events that led to our demise inside my brain since that day. Am I ready to unlock it all?

A giggling pair of girls stumbled into the kitchen, disrupting our heart-to-heart. I step back to create as much distance between Brynlee and myself as possible.

"I'll see you later." I said before bolting out of the room and into the sea of people.

I make my way towards Olivia when I notice she's alone.

"I see you got rid of the leech."

She rolls her eyes.

"What do you want, Reed?"

"A repeat of last summer, maybe?"

I must have had more alcohol than I thought as the words spewed from my mouth.

"What is wrong with you?"

Even in my semi-inebriated state, I can sense I touched a nerve.

Yet my rambling never ceased.

"Don't tell me you don't think about it," I said. "About *us.*"

My lip twitches at the sight of her creased brows. My stomach bubbles in anticipation of getting a reaction out of her. She takes a menacing step forward as I stare into her flaming eyes.

"Come near me again and I *will* taser you."

Her venomous words infiltrate my veins. I watch in disbelief as she stomps away through the crowd.

"Where have you been?" Marcus' voice drags me from my dubious thoughts.

"Wreaking havoc." I said. "Where have you been?"

He holds up his phone.

"Talking to Penelope."

I groan at the mention of *her* name. She has him whipped.

"There's a group of hot, single women and you're talking to your girlfriend that's miles away."

He raises his brows.

"That's what you do when you're in a committed relationship, Reed." He states as if it were general knowledge.

"That sounds boring." I said with a scoff. "Let's get you drunk."

I reach to grip his shoulder, but he moves back with his hands raised.

"You know I'm not doing that this summer."

I roll my eyes.

"How can I forget when you keep reminding me?" I scoff. "I'm relentless, though."

He chuckles.

"I couldn't describe you any better."

A boisterous yell echoes over the music as multiple heads turn toward the noise. I stifle a laugh as Connor stands on a table in nothing but his briefs, with a beer hat on his head. The crowd around him roars as he jumps into their awaiting arms. He cheers as he crowd surfs.

"When did he become so reckless?" I asked Marcus.

"Since he looked at you as a role model instead of his brothers."

I beam with pride.

"Maybe I should replace you."

He snorts.

"Good luck getting him to bail you out of trouble."

He has a point.

We have built our entire friendship on me getting into trouble, and Marcus coming to the rescue.

"Deny it all you want, but you wouldn't have it any other way."

Olivia

Reed Adler is an asshole. It's been a while since our confrontation, but I'm still fuming from his words.

How dare he bring up last summer?

I'd spent months pushing those memories to the back of my mind and he resurfaced it in a few seconds. *And he was smug about it, too.* I reached for a random bottle of alcohol and poured a shot. I regretted downing it the second it started burning my throat.

Tequila.

"That was brave of you," Wyatt speaks up as he enters through the threshold. "I've never been able to keep it down. I've always hated the taste."

My cheeks burn.

"I needed something strong."

"You made the right choice." He glances around the room as if he's paranoid about eavesdroppers. Once he's satisfied we're alone, he returns his attention to me. "Would you like to take a walk with me?"

I agreed. An intimate stroll on the beach at night.

What could be more romantic?

The moment we stepped out of the house and into the backyard of the beach, I gazed up at the sky. The sparkling stars stretch to infinity, calling on everyone to admire their beauty. I was awestruck by their simplistic charm.

"You know, I never planned to be attracted to anyone this summer."

I choked on my tongue at his boldness. I take a deep inhale to appear stoic.

"What could have changed your mind?"

He grins as if he's about to share a secret.

"I saw a girl taser this guy, and I was hooked."

I struggled to maintain my cool and bit my bottom lip to withhold my ear-splitting grin.

"I am pretty awesome."

He laughs.

"Don't forget modest."

Our blissful silence mixes with the rhythmic ripple of the waves to create the perfect euphony.

"So," I debate on whether to question him, but it is better I ask than to be left in doubt. "Why was the idea of a summer romance so unappealing?"

The terse silence swept over us like a tidal wave. He tucked his hands into his front pockets. His gaze is as far away as the endless sea.

"I just got out of a relationship before getting here."

Those words imploded my jovial mood. *I'm the rebound.*

"Were you together for long?"

"Since freshman year of high school."

Why not just deliver the knockout punch already?

"Why did you break up?" I asked but slapped myself for my insensitivity.

It's not like it's any of my business.

"We went to different colleges." He said. "The distance was too much to handle."

That's the worst breakup of all. There was no cheating. No falling out of love. I can tell by the tone of his voice that he's still in love with her. *Which sucks for me.*

The silence is unsettling. He clears his throat, but it does nothing to ease the heavy atmosphere.

"What about you?" He asked. "Any tragic romances?"

I release a humorless chuckle.

Tragic is a euphemism.

"There was someone last summer."

I didn't want to bring it up. I've tried placing last summer into the darkest crevice of my mind, but I'd pried in his non-existent love life, so it's only fair he asked too.

"What happened?"

I take a deep breath to gather my thoughts. To explain this without bringing up any tragic memories.

"Have you ever had that feeling you'd found the one?" I asked. "The one person you were destined to be with. Your forever. Only for them to turn out to be a raging douchebag?"

He chuckles at my words, but nods.

"That bad, huh?"

"That's an understatement."

We walk along the shore, bonded by our kindred heartbreak. It's comforting to know I'm not the only one with a broken-hearted story.

"You never told me how you feel."

I raise my brows as I tuck my hands further into my hoodie pockets. The frosty wind has picked up.

"About what?"

"About me."

He's bold. I'll give him that.

He glances at me with a tooth-achingly sweet smile. I drop my head, hoping he cannot see my scorching cheeks in the darkness.

"Does it matter?"

"I would hope so."

A part of me wanted to be honest and say he'd captured my attention, but the other part of me was warning me against the nauseating cliche. That the last guy to capture my attention left me wallowing in self-pity.

I promised myself a summer of no regrets.

"We both know I find you attractive." I said, biting the bullet. "I wouldn't take a late-night stroll with just anyone."

His dazzling smile has my heart doing somersaults.

"Now that we know we reciprocate our feelings, I suggest we take things one day at a time." He said. "Let's see how it goes with no pressure or labels."

I mull over his suggestion. It seems enticing. No pressure. Just the satisfaction of not having to feel alone all the time.

I weigh the pros and cons.

Are there any cons to this?

With that thought in mind, I nod my head in agreement.

"Sounds great to me."

He graced me with a toothy grin.

"How about we meet up tomorrow night?" He asked. "Have you been to the arcade?"

The mere mention of the arcade ignites an impulsive smile. A nest of nostalgia flickers through my mind. The hornets of memories are buzzing.

"The arcade is epic," I said. "I used to go with my brothers every summer when we were kids."

We'd spent our childhood in the arcade until we deemed ourselves *too old.* I never understood why, but I would give anything to go back again. Especially with Wyatt.

"Then it's a date."

A fleet of ships sail inside my stomach at the mention of a date - after last summer's disaster, I never walked into this summer with high expectations for romance. I would have never expected to meet Wyatt and like him so much in such a short amount of time. I'm not surprised. *Life is full of thrills and turmoil.*

7

Reed

My mind is as chaotic as high tide. My thoughts roll in and out, gliding to the surface before retreating. I blame the abundance of alcohol. I tumble as I walk along the shore, kicking the sand and clutching the bottle of vodka in my hand. There are only a few drops left.

I sway the bottle back and forth as a few drops jump out and dissolve into the sand, humming a random tune as I journey into the unknown. I do not know where I'm going, but my legs seem adamant about walking.

Harmonious laughter echoes along the shore. I glance ahead with hazy eyes, making out the pair in the distance. My steps hastened.

As I got closer, I noticed their familiar faces. I watch Olivia giggling as *the jerkoff* twirls her around. She spins like a ballerina before bursting into an onslaught of laughter. His grating laughter follows. I roll my eyes at the nauseating scene before me. I hear footsteps crunching the sand behind me, but I don't tear my gaze away.

"What are you doing?" Marcus asked.

I take a deep sip of my drink before replying.

"Taking in the view."

My buzz is wearing off.

"It's gorgeous, isn't it?" he asked, gazing out into the dark abyss of the ocean as if I were talking about the moon.

If only.

My eyes burn at the romantic interaction, but it's like watching a horror movie. It's gory, but I can't look away. Like some psychological thriller. I tear my eyes away and chug the remaining liquid, wincing before tossing the bottle into the sand.

"I've seen better."

I turn my back on the vulgar sight and stumble along the sand, nearly falling face-first. Good thing Marcus has quick reflexes.

"I thought we would not make a habit of this." He reprimands me, but the smile on his face assures me he's only half-serious.

"I'll try harder next time."

Could I be any more disingenuous?

"You say that every time."

"One day I'll mean it."

Alcohol always seems like a good idea. Until the next morning. A hangover is like an invisible torture weapon. The inability to muster the strength to leave my bed, the unquenchable thirst, and my inflated brain were ready to burst any second.

It always gets the best of me. I strain my eyes as I turn to glance at the clock beside me. *I slept through the entire morning.*

A knock on my door amplified the pain in my head.

"What?"

"Good morning to you too." Marcus sticks his head in. "I came to check if you were still breathing."

"Barely."

He chuckles and huddles further into the room.

"Anyone indecent in here?"

"Just you."

He bites his bottom lip, but the upturn of the corners makes it known he found it humorous.

"I have a solution to your hangover." He said. "How about a friendly one on one?"

The suggestion was the magic cure. Enough to give me the strength to lift myself into an upright position.

"Are you sure?" I asked. "Even with a hangover, I could kick your ass."

He chuckles.

"I'm not scared."

During our off seasons, we'd practice at the local rink to stay in shape. Ever since we were kids, we'd compete against each other as often as we could. It always frustrated Marcus that he could never beat me, but I couldn't be happier.

Hockey is my sole area of expertise.

"I accept your challenge."

It's as if something has miraculously cured my hangover. The idea of winning against Marcus in a *friendly* game is more tempting than sulking in bed. I exit my bedroom and am greeted by hushed voices down the hallway. I knit my brows and tiptoe to Olivia's door, pressing my ear against it.

"We're going out to the arcade tonight." She squeals in excitement.

A girlish gasp breaks free from under the door. *Chelsea.*

"We need to ensure perfection."

I roll my eyes at their generic conversation.

"He's so perfect." Olivia swoons. I resist the urge to vomit. "And he's a musician."

Musicians are overrated.

"It makes him even more attractive!" Olivia said. "I have a thing for musicians."

I scrunch my nose in disgust at their nauseating obsessing and push myself away from the door. *There are more important things than spying on them.*

I have perfect clarity every time I glide along the ice. The familiarity brings me comfort and an unshakeable confidence as I push my legs in haste to out-skate Marcus. I hit the puck into the net before he could even defend. I raise my hands in victory.

"No one likes a pretentious jock."

"No one likes a loser either."

"You should be used to losing." An infuriating voice pipes in.

Wyatt skates towards us with his entourage shadowing him.

"With that attitude, you should be used to being punched in the face," I said. "I know I've enjoyed taking a few shots."

My words drag his smug grin down.

Good. You jackass.

"You think you're better than everyone else, Adler." He said with clenched fists. "You've never been able to beat me in any games since sophomore year of high school."

I know he's trying to rile me up. I hate that it's working.

"You talk about a big game," I said. "Why not prove it?"

"I don't have to prove anything." He said. "Also, you're on my ice, so I'd choose my next words wisely."

"This doesn't belong to you."

"It does now." His arrogant grin makes my blood boil. "My dad just bought the place."

The St. James family has made no secret of their wealth, so I shouldn't be surprised.

"It's a good thing your daddy is rich."

"Why's that?"

"He can afford to pay for your medical bills after I kick your ass."

I charged for him, but Marcus could read my thoughts better than anyone else. He blocked me before I could move an inch. I tried to break from his hold, but he's gotten skilled at holding me back from an altercation.

"He's not worth it." Marcus whispers.

It would be worth watching his face crack under my fist.

Wyatt delivers a condescending wink before skating to the other side of the rink with his tailing idiots.

"I hate that guy."

"Me too."

I clench my jaw.

"Why didn't you let me punch him if you hate him too?"

He sighs and drags his fingers through his locks.

"I wouldn't do that to Olivia."

His reasoning unsettles me. My fists clench at my sides as I scowl in Wyatt's direction. He's glancing at his phone with a wide grin, and I grind my teeth at the possibility of who he could be talking to. My face is flushed as I fight with the devil and angel on my shoulder. The devil urges revenge, the angel urges restraint. *I always had difficulty resisting sin.*

"Let's go to the arcade tonight."

My mouth spews traitorous words before I can stop it.

"Why?"

I feign indifference. As if I weren't plotting revenge. As if I weren't about to sabotage his sister's date.

"It's been a while," I said. "It would be fun."

He contemplates my suggestion and shrugs.

"Let's do it."

Olivia

I'd been pacing for ten minutes. I shake my sweaty palms at my side as I burn a hole in the wooden floor. *He's late.* My throat feels dry.

I march downstairs as my summer dress sways around me and enter the crowded kitchen. My brothers, Reed and Chelsea, are standing around the counter munching on a bag of nacho chips.

"I'm so glad you chose that dress." Chelsea grins.

Their heads turn toward me.

"Why do you look like that?" Connor asked before shoving a chip full of guacamole into his mouth.

"I have a date."

Marcus freezes.

"With who?"

My heart thumps as I make eye contact with Chelsea. Her eyes are as wide as mine.

"Wyatt."

I don't know what reaction I expected from him. *Panic? Anger?*

He sighs, not taking his gaze off me.

"Have fun."

I gaze at him as if waiting for him to deliver the punchline. In his eyes, this would be my first date in forever. I'd only dated two guys in my life - and Marcus was only aware of one.

"Thank you."

I run my fingers through my hair. The air is thick with tension. My eyes gaze around the room. Reed broke the tension as he launched out of his seat, placed his plate in the sink, and stormed out.

What's his deal?

The doorbell chimes throughout the house, and my heart palpitates. I wipe my clammy hands on my dress and Chelsea rushes over to fix my hair. Once I feel presentable enough, I speed-walk towards the front door. Bile rises in my throat as Reed beats me to it and opens the door for Wyatt. He leans against the doorframe, blocking Wyatt from entering.

"May I help you?" Reed asked.

Even with his back turned to me, I could sense his smug grin. His shoulders stiffen as he folds them across his chest.

"I'm here for Olivia."

"Well, that's unfortunate for her."

I decided it was time to intervene and marched toward the pair. I hit Reed's back. He glances at me over his shoulder.

"That's enough."

He raises his hand in surrender and bites the corner of his lip.

"Have her back by midnight." Reed reprimanded and pointed an accusatory finger in Wyatt's direction. "Not a moment later."

I watch him jog up the stairs and wait until his footsteps are distant enough before turning to Wyatt.

"I'm sorry about him."

"It's okay. No one knows better than me how maddening Reed Adler can be."

I shrug.

"I'm stuck with him."

It's the truth. Reed had always been there. He and Marcus have been inseparable ever since the day they met. As much as I dislike Reed, I knew he would walk through hell and back for Marcus. He was the brother he had never had.

We'd become the family he never had.

Wyatt clears his throat, pulling me from the nostalgic longing for the simpler times.

"Are you ready to go?"

I nod my head and follow him out the door.

The high spirits of the arcade seeped into my blood like a shot of Adrenaline. The cachinnated laughter of the children filled my eardrums as they dragged their parents along to the various games.

A hurricane of memories flooded my mind. How we'd drag our parents everywhere, eager to get from game to game. We'd always have a competition to see who could end the night with the most tickets.

I think back to a specific night when Marcus, Connor, and Reed teamed up and put their tickets together. I'd sobbed for twenty minutes straight to my mom about how they *cheated.* Eli felt so sorry for me that he gave me all his tickets.

It was the first time I'd ever won a competition against the boys.

My heart clenches as the memory makes me miss Eli more than I already do. He'd always been on my side. Marcus always joked that I was his favorite, but underneath the humor, I always believed it to be true.

"Any game you want to try first?"

Wyatt brings me back to conscious reality.

"I'm a champion at Skee-Ball."

He gazes at me. His grin is challenging.

"I guess it's champion versus champion."

With a wicked grin, I strutted toward the Skee-Ball area, surprised to find it vacant. My competitive nature takes over, as my only goal is beating Wyatt. I hold the ball in both hands, rubbing it like a genie lamp. It's how I get into *the zone*. I pull my arm back before launching.

40 points.

"Not a poor start."

He reaches for his own ball and gazes at his target with pursed lips before letting it go.

30 points.

I gaze at him with a self-approving grin.

"Don't get too confident." He said. "We're just getting started."

8

Reed

I scrunch my face at the annoying sound of children's laughter. Their banshee wails are like nails on a chalkboard. I rub my temples as a group of kids runs around me like annoying ants.

If only I could stomp on them.

It's no secret I'm not the biggest fan of kids.

"What are we doing first?" Connor slides between Marcus and me. He rubs his hands together as he scopes the surroundings. "I could eat."

I rolled my eyes at his unwavering love for food, but my stomach couldn't help but agree.

All the intoxicating scents are too delectable to resist. I have an immense craving for extra cheesy nachos.

The three of us went our separate ways, agreeing to meet up at the benches once we'd gotten our orders. I tap my foot as I wait in line. I jumped out of my skin as a pair of arms slithered around my waist, followed by grating laughter.

"Hey." Alyssa purrs.

"Hi."

I take a step to the side to create as much of a distance as possible without leaving the line.

"I didn't expect to see you here tonight."

I was hoping you'd never see me again. I wanted to voice my thoughts aloud, but I bit my tongue instead.

"I haven't been here in ages," I said. "Spending quality time with Marcus and Connor."

I brought it up in hopes she'd get the hint that our conversation should end so I could get back to my friends. Her smile widens.

"I should say hi to them."

I close my eyes and take a deep breath through my nostrils. *All I wanted was some nachos.* Forgoing my nachos, I tuck my hands in my front pockets and stalk off, knowing she'd follow me. Her footsteps shadow mine. Marcus and Connor have taken their seats. They littered the table with a variety of foods.

"Look who's here."

I slouch in the seat next to Marcus and lean my elbows up on the table, placing my chin in my hands. I drone out their conversation as my eyes glance around at all the games. All the memories of summer's past clogged my mind. I glanced at the Skee-Ball area and spotted Wyatt with Olivia. My desire for revenge reawakened as his smug face boiled my blood. *The douchebag is wearing a sweater vest.* They talk momentarily before he strolls off, leaving her alone. I launch out of my seat without excusing myself and march towards her like a lion on its prey.

"What a strange coincidence seeing you here."

She turns around and her eyes widen in disbelief.

"What are *you* doing here?" She asked.

Her eyes are drowning in hatred.

"Was craving some nachos."

She scrunches her nose in disgust and folds her arms across her chest.

"Leave now before I taser you."

My corner lip twitches.

"You're so sexy when you're angry."

Her nostrils flare as I grin in satisfaction. It's the exact reaction I wanted out of her.

"Now isn't the time to play the jealous ex-boyfriend."

My smile dropped. Her words were like a torpedo to my gut. I square my shoulders and inhale to regain my composure.

"I'm not playing."

I step forward and bend until my lips are right by her ear. Her breath hitches at our proximity.

"If I can remember correctly, this is where we had our first date," I whispered. "You loved it when I wrapped my arms around you as we played Skee-Ball. I showed you how to get a high score every time." I bit off a smirk. "You loved a lot of the things I did for *and to* you."

Neither of us moved. Nothing escaped our lips besides our jagged breaths. I beam with pride at rendering her speechless. However, my satisfaction was short-lived. I lose my footing as she shoves me with every ounce of strength. I tumble backward and grip a table for support.

Flames are alight in her eyes. The metaphorical embers project her hatred for me.

"Those days are over. *We're* over." She said. "You made sure of that."

Olivia

There was a time when Reed Adler was my entire world. When I used to believe that we were forever. Destined for an epic and infinite romance. However, destiny is a fallacy. Just like *true love*. I gave Reed Adler my heart, only for him to break it and return it before the warranty ended. A love that was believed to be *forever* couldn't even survive a summer. He always had a way of getting under my skin, making me want to punch him and then kiss the bruise better.

We never get over our first love. As much as I hate to admit it, a piece of my heart will forever be his. However, it's time to walk away with the remaining pieces. *It's time to walk away from him.*

Something had distracted me ever since our altercation. Wyatt must have noticed, as he pulled me out of my rampant thoughts by placing his hand on my shoulder.

"Are you okay?" he asked with furrowed brows.

I shake my jaded thoughts from my mind and muster a smile.

"I'm great."

His tender smile makes my heart flutter. He reaches for my hand and folds his fingers between mine. My heart hums against my chest and my cheeks feel as if they might combust.

It's like I'm in middle school again.

We stroll around the arcade in search of something else to do. We swing our hands back and forth before deciding on playing a few more games. Our competitive nature took over, as we were both adamant about beating the other. He made me laugh the entire time, so much so that my stomach ached. It was like a cheesy Romcom. I despised the genre, but that it was happening to me made it a new favorite.

"It's been a while since I've had so much fun." Wyatt voices my thoughts.

Our interlocked hands sway as we stroll along the promenade. The gentle breeze brushed past, littering my arms with goosebumps. I inhaled the fragrant ocean scent.

"Thank you for making this so much fun."

We halt underneath the hundreds of lights along the promenade. It might just be my imagination, but the light made his eyes sparkle. *Perhaps I've gotten too into the Romcom mindset.*

"I wouldn't have had as much fun with anyone else."

There's an indistinguishable look in his eyes. It feels like there's a marching band in my stomach, playing in tangent to my throbbing heart.

Wyatt leans in and my breath hitches in nervous anticipation. *He'd be the second guy I've ever kissed.* His lips on mine felt foreign but inviting. His hands glide from my shoulders and place themselves on my hips. An angelic melody hums within as I dissolve into the soft kiss.

We parted but remained close enough that I could feel his warm breath mix with mine. His smile is contagious as we stand like a bunch of lovesick fools. Yet I couldn't give a damn about what others thought. *It's time to be reckless.*

For the first time in forever, I woke up ready to seize the day. Not even an army could defeat the war inside my stomach. I skipped down the steps.

"Morning."

Chelsea, Connor, and Marcus are standing around the table. Connor shoves pancakes into his mouth like a squirrel gathering for the winter. Marcus glances at him in disgust. I couldn't blame him. Chelsea always had a flair for cooking. I grab a few pancakes for myself before Connor devours the pile. I layer them in golden syrup as Reed enters with bowed shoulders. He rubs his eyes.

"Where have you been?" Marcus asked. "I came to check on you this morning and you weren't in your room."

"I was out."

He slides a gift bag to me over the counter. I raise my brows and step back as if something is going to jump out at me.

"I found it on the doorstep." He said. "Has your name on it."

All eyes are on me as I glance at the tag. It's a generic card with my name printed on it. My heart hums as I unveil a fluffy bear clutching a heart. Chelsea mimics my reaction. I turn the card over.

I should have won this for you last night.

"Wyatt is the sweetest."

I passed the card to Chelsea so she could read it.

"I've never felt more single."

"How do you know it's from him?" Reed asked.

I squint at him as if it were the dumbest question ever. *For Reed, that's an accomplishment.*

"Who else would send her a bear, dumbass?"

Chelsea sneered before I could get a word out. *My response would have been similar.*

"It was just a question."

I roll my eyes at his attitude before admiring the bear. Its eyes may be a dull black, but it seemed to sparkle as bright as Wyatt's.

I'm going to cherish it.

9

Reed

Why did I not sign my name on that fucking card? If I did, she wouldn't be worshiping the ground that *jerkoff* walks on.

He gets to take the credit for my idea.

I spent the entire night gathering tickets, even bribing an eight-year-old to give me his. I gave the little demon fifty bucks.

All that for Wyatt St. James to get the glory.

I exited the room, hoping I was inconspicuous. I couldn't listen to another second of Olivia fawning over that douchebag.

I have no right to be jealous.

Despite it all, I can't help but feel fury at the thought of him with her. Of *anyone* with her. However, it's no one else's fault but mine that we're over. I messed up and I doubt anything I do will fix it.

I slammed the garage door and leaned against it, gripping my hair in my hands as I inhaled and exhaled to calm my erratic breaths. I'd always had trouble controlling my emotions, but the control had jumped out the window. I glance around the room for a distraction when my eyes land on something covered by a burgundy sheet. The shape looks familiar. I grip the edge of the sheet and toss it to the side.

My old drum set.

It's been years since I've played. It had been an outlet for my frustration, but I'd abandoned it the moment I took hockey seriously. My hands itched to play again. I wanted to pretend it was for a sense of nostalgia, but I can't deny my true motives. A part of me wants to impress *her.* The same way she's impressed by *him.*

Bile rises in my throat as I compare myself to *Wyatt St. James*. As much as I hate to admit it. I envy him. He was her knight in shining armor when I was the dragon imprisoning her. He swooped in on my fatal error. As much as I try to say goodbye to her. To us. I can never forget the good times.

I get to work wiping years' worth of dust off the tattered instrument. Once it's spotless, I step back and admire its brand-new shine.

"What are you doing?" Marcus asked.

"Found this old beauty."

"I haven't seen this in years." He chuckled. "You used it to impress girls."

I snorted at how gullible I was as a freshman.

"Until I found out hockey was the key all along."

He scoffs.

"What made you want to play again?"

My shoulders stiffen as I tighten my fists at my side.

"No reason."

I try to keep my breathing as steady as possible. My stomach clenches as the unbearable guilt eats at my stomach like radioactive acid. I hate lying to Marcus. He shrugs and pats my back.

"I'll let you get back to it." He said. "See you later for some training."

Once he shuts the door behind him, I tune the set. The memories translate into my brain. *Like riding a bicycle.* I take a deep breath and shake my shoulders, gripping the sticks in my hand. I'm a little rusty, but with a bit more practice, it will all come back to me. *It has to.*

Olivia

I've been on cloud nine ever since this morning. I haven't moved from my bed as I gaze up at the ceiling with the bear clutched in my arms. The knock on my door is barely noticeable through my daydreaming.

"Come in!" I called.

Chelsea enters the room and flops next to me, mimicking my action of glancing at the ceiling. She says nothing. The only sounds are our heavy breathing and my ceiling fan. She sighs before turning her head to me.

"Have you texted him?"

I shake my head.

"I don't want to seem too eager."

She nods.

"Love is complicated." She said.

"I couldn't agree more."

"You know what would make you feel better?"

"What?"

"Ice cream."

I turn to her with a grin. I love how she knows me.

"That sounds perfect."

I sit up and stretch my arms over my head.

"Then we can't waste another second."

Golden fingers of sunlight tickled my skin as I scooped another decadent spoonful of chocolate mint ice cream into my mouth. I moan in delight. The blue sky was dotted with fluffy clouds, reminding me of sheep. I watched as they drifted in the gentle breeze. I feel another burning against my face. Not from the sun, but from Chelsea's piercing gaze.

"What?" I asked and self-consciously brushed my cheek. "Did I get something on my face?"

"Nothing." She said with a creepy smile. "It's just good to see you happy again."

I drop my head. She reaches over the table and places her hand on mine.

"Last year was tough on you." She said. "You've been so brave, and you deserve this."

My lips twitch as my eyes prickle with tears.

"Last year was tough on all of us." I sniffled. "I know it wasn't easy on you either. To watch me go through that."

She holds back a sob and inhales a shaky breath.

"It was the worst time of my life." She said. "But none of that matters anymore because you're *here*. *We're* here together eating this delicious ice cream."

I squeeze her hand in appreciation. She always knew the right things to say. So much has changed since last summer. It feels like a lifetime ago.

129

My toes curl as we step onto the sandy beach. It's as soft as cotton candy. I gaze up as a flock of seagulls fly over our heads, squawking and squabbling over something in one's beak. I inhale the earthy air. It's the perfect therapy.

"What's the plan for tonight?" Chelsea asked as we dipped our toes in the water.

"I have no idea."

"There's got to be a party somewhere."

I roll my eyes. Parties have always been her priority. Any excuse to mingle. She nudges me with a grin.

"What about Wyatt?" She asked.

"What about him?"

"Hasn't he texted?"

I bite my lip and gaze at my painted toenails.

"I haven't heard from him since our date."

I didn't want to text him for fear of looking desperate, but anxious thoughts swarmed in my mind.

Did I do something wrong?

Why would he send me a bear the next day if he wanted nothing to do with me?

I know I'm overthinking everything, but my brain is cursed. No matter how many times I tell myself to calm down, my thoughts deceive me. I had been on cloud nine only for it to burst.

"We need something to distract you." Chelsea said as we strolled along the shore.

The sand is a gentle hue of gold. The coastline is an amalgamation of sea and sky - a covenant of immortal beauty.

She gasps and hits my arm.

"Ow!" I exclaim, rubbing the tender spot.

I bruise easily.

"Let's have our own party!"

I gaze at her as if she'd suggested we swim with the sharks.

"Have you forgotten about Marcus?" I asked. "He's become a fun sucker. He'd never allow it."

She gazes at me. Her cerulean eyes have turned darker, and her familiar twisted smile appears.

"Who says we have to tell him?"

I knew it was a bad idea the moment Chelsea suggested it, yet I did nothing to stop it. She has made a lot of friends in the short time she's been here, considering our home is at maximum capacity.

I dread the moment Marcus gets home.

I shiver at the thought but shrug it off. Everyone's already here, so I might as well enjoy it. I pour a generous amount of vodka into my soda and take a sip. The burn is unbelievably satisfying.

My eyes lock with Wyatt's and I try my best to remain casual despite the stampede of my heart. He rushes over and embraces me in a comforting hug. I inhale his delicious scent.

"You made it!"

His presence surprises me. *It seems Chelsea has been scheming again.*

"I was hoping to see you."

Those simple words and gentle gaze were enough to put my mind at ease. It was the exact reassurance I needed from him. The blissful moment becomes shattered as a random couple enters the room. One of them trips and pulls the other down with them. They crack up.

"Want to talk outside?" Wyatt whispers in my ear.

I nod. He grips my hand in his and leads me through the bunched-up crowd and out onto the back porch. It was far less crowded, which I was grateful for. I led him to the outdoor seating my mom set up to go with her garden.

Her little landscaping hobby.

We sit next to each other and our thighs brush against each other. I look away, hoping to hide my reddening cheeks as his natural warmth seeps into my veins and into my heart.

The night sky is picturesque, the dark sky is the ultimate backdrop for the full moon. It shines that you can almost see every crater. It demands attention, making the surrounding stars seem dull.

"You look beautiful, by the way."

I turned to him. We're so close together that I can see every intricate detail in his eyes. I admire the swirls of honey I'd never noticed before.

"Thank you," I whispered. "And thank you for the flowers."

He clears his throat and glances toward the house.

"Oh, you're welcome." He said as he glanced at his feet. "So, what made you decide to host a party?"

I pick at the paint on my nails.

"I didn't. It was all Chelsea's idea."

"You both seem pretty close."

I smile at his observation. *Close is an understatement.*

"She's the sister I never had," I said. "We met in second grade, and we've been inseparable ever since."

"Let me guess. You plan everything together?"

"We'd chosen colleges by the time we were ten. We made a pact that we'd be roommates and everything."

He chuckles and leans further in the seat.

"What are you planning on majoring in?"

"I've always wanted to be a veterinarian." My smile widens at the thought. "It's been my dream for as long as I can remember."

"That's impressive." He said. "Smart and beautiful. I sure am a lucky guy."

My entire body malfunctioned. I hadn't realized I'd been holding my breath until my lungs burned. He places one hand on my knee and draws my head closer to his with the other. His lips engulf mine apprehensively, as if he's trying to gauge my reaction. Once I show no sign of objection, he deepens the kiss. I could feel the faint tickle of his breath as he glided his fingers through my hair. We breathe each other in, only momentarily breaking apart before attaching our lips together again. Every kiss is getting better. *I could do this all night.*

10

Reed

For a moment, I thought we'd stepped into the wrong house. The blaring music reached miles away. I thought it was the neighbors, but the intoxicated teens running out of our house to puke in a nearby bush gave it away. I glance at Marcus. His face is as red as a tomato. If this were an animation, he'd have the cliche smoke out of his ears.

The girls are in big trouble.

He shoves through the herd as Connor, and I struggle to keep up with his haste. He pushes past the crowd like they're human bowling pins, knocking them back with one strike. Connor gets distracted by a group of people lounging around in the corner, leaving me to shadow Marcus. I grip his arm.

"You look upstairs, and I'll look down here," I said. "That way, we can cover more ground."

He gnaws on his bottom lip before nodding. He's too frustrated to voice his thoughts. I watched him stomp upstairs before searching for the pair of troublemakers. I venture outside knowing Olivia often ventures outside to escape the buzz of a party. She could only handle it for so long before she'd get bored.

It's less crowded outside. I spotted her immediately. My stomach churns at the sight of her lips locked with Wyatt's. Anger scorched my body, seeping through my skin and into my veins. I dig my nails into the palm of my hands, not caring that I'm piercing the surface. My jaw feels as if it's about to snap. Twisted thoughts poison my mind like venom.

A million ways to murder Wyatt St. James and make it look like an accident.

My mind escaped me at that moment, as if the ocean breeze had blown it away, leaving my head uninhabited. It's as if someone else had taken control, luring me to imminent trouble. Before I could register my movements, I'd already walked towards the control box for the sprinklers. I flipped it on.

Olivia shrieks at the unexpected moisture, breaking *his* hold on her. I wanted to gloat in satisfaction, but it did nothing to ease my frustrations. He gripped her hand and dragged her out of the danger zone. I ran my fingers through my hair before stomping back into the house before anyone could see me. I speed-walk to the kitchen, but I'm blocked by Marcus.

"Did you find her?"

"Nope."

I reach for a random bottle of vodka, wasting no time in unscrewing the lid and chugging the contents. I revel in the burn as it numbs my rage. It dries up my throat, but I drink more. *I need more.*

My eyes fall on Alyssa, or more her outfit. She has left little to the imagination, but I'm not complaining. I scope her out as she strolls up to me.

"I've been looking for you." She said.

"Any reason in particular?"

She bites her bottom lip and places her hand on my chest. Our eye contact never wavers as she slides her hand down my chest until she halts above my penis. I fight the urge, but I respond to her caress. She leans on her tiptoes and stretches until her lips brush against my earlobe.

"Let's go somewhere quieter and I'll tell you."

The moment I glance at her mischievous, red-coated lips, I lose all inhibition. I'm dragging her upstairs at record speed. I shut the door before I shoved her against it. Our bodies pressed together. My tongue pressed between her parted lips as we fumbled to take off one another's clothes. I wrap her legs around me, not breaking the kiss, and rush to my bed. I drop her on the mattress and hover over her for another hungry kiss. We groan into each other's mouths as my hardened length brushes against her bare thigh. She grabs my hair on the back of my head, drawing me closer.

I pull away to catch my breath before reaching over to grab a condom from my nightstand. I was in no mood for foreplay.

This wasn't for love or for romance. As shallow as it may seem, this is for pleasure. A way for me to release pent-up frustration. A way for me to forget about all my issues and my deadly thoughts.

I don't love Alyssa. I barely *like* her. There's no passion. No desire. All because the one I truly want is in the arms of another and I have no one else but myself to blame.

This is nothing but a distraction.

I woke up to insipid music booming throughout the house. The party hasn't seemed to die down. The generous moonlight provides the only source of light in my room. I lift myself, knocking someone's hand off me. I glance at the platinum messy locks and resist the urge to scrunch my nose, bolting out of the bed as if a python was inside, and put on my clothes. I glance at her once more to make sure she's still asleep before tiptoeing outside.

"I've done a few *walk of shames* in my life, but never from my house."

The voice makes me jump out of my skin. Brynlee is leaning against the wall with a smug grin. She folds her arms across her chest and tilts her head to the side as if she's waiting for my excuse.

"There's no shame here."

The corner of her lip twitches.

"Want to have a drink with me?" She asked.

"Why not?" The kitchen is vacant and I'm thankful for the momentary bliss. "What's your poison?"

"Vodka."

She hoists herself onto the counter and kicks her dangling legs back and forth. I slide the drink over to her, waiting in anticipation to hear her deliberation.

"Fantastic."

I fixed a drink of my own before leaning over the counter beside her. The obnoxious music and drunk partiers disturbed our silence. I can feel her eyes on me, but I keep mine on my drink. Her stare is searing into the side of my head.

"What?"

She lifts her glass to her lips to mask her smile.

"Nothing," she said. "You just seem to have a lot on your mind."

I shake my head.

"Not really."

She shrugs and takes a small sip of her half-empty drink. She twirls her glass in her hand as the ice keeps hitting the edges. I gaze at her from the corner of my eye, but she's focused on her glass.

"Something on your mind?" I asked.

She stops all movement but doesn't speak. Her faraway gaze doesn't waver, not even when I step closer.

"I was in love once."

Her gaze remains on the wall as if she's in a hypnotic trance.

Her confession has taken me by surprise. Where is this coming from? I had a million questions for her, but I figure she'll elaborate when she's ready. I lifted my glass to my lips to find it empty, but I didn't want to move to refill it in case she felt I wasn't listening or didn't care.

"I'd felt nothing so real before." She said. "And I ruined it."

Her eyes are glossy as she looks into mine.

"How did you do that?"

"By being my destructive self."

I cower under her gaze, not liking the way she's looking at me.

With pity.

"You remind me so much of myself."

Her words are like a slap in the face, especially after her confession.

"What are you talking about?"

"We both run away from anything real."

I flinch. Her words did not bother me. I didn't care if her words were laced with judgment, I cared more that it carried truth.

"You've lost me."

She scoffs.

"This thing you have going on with Alyssa, it's all a distraction from the one thing you truly want." She said. "The one thing you don't think you deserve."

She chugs the remaining contents in her glass and pulls a face as if she'd just sucked a lemon.

"I know the signs." She continues. "You don't think you deserve love, or that you're worthy of it. So, you do whatever you can to push it away."

As much as I wanted to deny it and tell her it's all nothing but bullshit - a part of me knows she's right. It's been my curse. My fatal flaw.

The moment something in my life feels blissful - I run. I'd never allowed myself to fall in love or to be vulnerable to anyone. It's always been my biggest and only rule. Avoid love at all costs.

Until last summer.

She swept me off my feet and stole my heart in one fell swoop. It was the most genuine and epic feeling I'd ever experienced. Like a newborn seeing the world for the first time. It was as if my eyes and heart had been locked until she showed up with the key.

Until I ruined it.

She reached over and placed her hand on top of mine.

"Promise me you won't make the same mistake I did."

I drop my head.

"It's too late. I already have."

She squeezes my hand. I glance at her from under my lashes, wanting to shove my head in the oven.

"Never count yourself out." She said. "Epic love always comes back. You just need to fight for it."

11

Olivia

It's amazing how quickly three weeks can pass when you're having fun. This summer has already lived up to its hype and there's still more to come. Penelope, Marcus' girlfriend, is arriving today to spend the rest of the summer with us and I couldn't be more excited.

She's perfect for Marcus and he's happiest around her. It's also a plus that he could focus his attention on her instead of fussing over me. I'm craving freedom.

I skip down the stairs as I hum a random tune in my head. It's familiar, but I can't place a name on it. However, a conflicting tune booms over my melody. I venture toward the sound. The closer I get, the more coherent it becomes.

It's the sound of drumming.

I stand outside the garage door and peer my head into the room.

Reed is beating the sticks against the snare of the drums. It has been ages since I've seen him go anywhere near his drum kit.

My mom bought it for him one summer. We could never figure out why, considering it was nowhere near his birthday or Christmas, but she always treated Reed as if he were her own.

"It's rude to spy, Olive."

I was so entrapped in my thoughts that I didn't notice he'd stopped drumming.

"I had to see what that noise was that's disturbing the neighborhood."

He grins but doesn't move from behind his set.

"You're just upset because you're insanely attracted to me right now." He said. "Admit it, Olive, this image does it for you."

He leans forward with the sticks in his hands. The corner of his lip rises as his eyes trail the length of my body. His black shirt strains against his biceps. I furrow my brows and fold my arms across my chest.

He wishes.

"I have no idea what you're talking about."

He lifts himself from his seat and struts around the drum set with an infuriating amount of confidence and leans down until his lips are near my ear. His cologne invades my scent.

"Your eyes always had a way of deceiving you, Olive."

He pulls away and gazes into my eyes. His sparkle with mischief. He chuckles to himself as if he'd had the funniest thought before brushing past me, leaving his lingering scent.

I stood comatose in the middle of the room until the shrill screaming of Chelsea revived my mind. I shake myself off before rushing toward the noise. I find Chelsea and Penelope bouncing from left to right as they hug. Penelope's eyes lock with mine over Chelsea's shoulder.

"Ollie!"

She breaks from the hug before rushing toward me. I accept her embrace. Penelope has been the big sister I've always wanted, and I missed her.

"I've missed you so much."

I squeezed her tighter.

"Not as much as I missed you."

We pull apart, and I take the moment to admire her subtle changes in appearance. She cut her blonde locks a few inches shorter, but it complimented her flawless face.

Before I could compliment her, arms encircled her waist as Marcus spun her around in his arms. Her giggles fill the room even when he sets her down. He doesn't waste a moment to attach his lips to hers. As disturbing as it is, I can't help but smile. They're perfect for each other. I've never seen him so happy.

I envy their love.

Someone's groan disrupts their affectionate display.

"Do you have to do that in front of everyone?"

Penelope's face falls along with mine.

"Hello, *Reed.*"

"Penelope."

He leans against the entryway with his arm above his head. She scrunches her nose in distaste before turning back to Marcus.

"What's the plan for today?"

"I have an entire day planned for us."

He beams with pride. I catch the roll of Reed's eyes before he strides into the kitchen. My phone buzzes in my back pocket and I can't help but smile as Wyatt's name appears on the screen.

Want to hang out today?

My fingers hover over the screen as I try to think of a cute and witty reply, yet all I could muster was, *of course.* My heart flutters as he types a response. Most guys would wait a while to seem in control and carefree. *Not Wyatt.* He always makes me feel appreciated.

Pick you up in an hour.

I resist the urge to squeal and draw attention to myself. This moment is about Penelope's return. Yet, she and Marcus are so loved up that they won't even notice if I'm gone.

Reed

And just like that, my plans for a fun-filled summer have combusted and I'm left with ashes of disappointment. That's the effect Penelope has on Marcus.

If he wasn't the biggest stickler for the rules before, he sure is now.

The Dementor of fun.

"I've been looking for you," Connor said, entering the kitchen. "Did you know Penelope is here?"

"How could I not? Everything's grim."

He rolls his eyes with a slight smile.

"Well, since Marcus is out, why don't we hang out?"

"What do you have in mind?"

He leans across the counter with a mischievous grin that puts mine to shame.

Connor Huxley is pure trouble and I'm here for it.

"I'm thinking of getting a tattoo."

The wheel in my brain gets stuck for a moment as if it was rusted before I erupt in laughter.

"Your mom would kill you."

Mrs. Huxley despised tattoos. She never said why, but I remember when I came home with my first tattoo and she lectured me for an hour before trying to scrub it off with a sponge, thinking it was fake. She eventually got over it, but I think she'd die of a stroke if her own child came home with one.

"She's not here."

I know I should convince him to back out. Tell him it's an awful idea and we should grab food instead.

However, I've never been the voice of reason. Let the chaos ensue.

"Well, let's get going."

❁

The regret magnifies in his eyes the moment we enter the tattoo parlor. I bite off a smile and pat his shoulder. He gazes at me like a lost child asking me to help find their mother.

"It's not too late to back out."

"Is it painful?"

"Excruciating."

I couldn't help but chuckle at the ambivalence of the situation. A part of me feels guilty for trying to scare him, but the other part is reveling in the twisted mental torture. He mumbles to himself as if trying to hype himself up.

"I can do this."

I gently shoved him forward.

"You've got this, buddy."

He stops in his tracks. His eyes were firmly set on something, or rather *someone*. A girl is standing behind the counter. The pink stripes in her shoulder-length brunette hair immediately demand attention. The chestnut amplified the hot pink. Her lip ring sparkles under the harsh light. Connor maneuvers toward her. I roll my eyes, not wanting to get in his way.

"Are you looking to get another one?" One of the employee's questions.

He's a stocky man with a beard that seems to almost touch his gut. I glance down at my left arm, already littered with an array of ink.

"Why not?"

I'm already here.

"You got something in mind?"

I think back on all the possibilities. There was one I'd wanted to get for a while, but I don't think it would be appropriate.

No one would know.

"Yeah, there's one I've been thinking of getting, but I'm not too sure if now's the right time for it."

"There's no time like now."

I couldn't help but agree. I glance at myself in the full-length mirror.

"I'm thinking of having it done above my heart."

I place my hand on the area.

"What do you have in mind?"

"A date," I said. "July 14th."

He shrugs as if he gets this kind of request every day. *He probably does.*

"Let's get started."

Connor couldn't stop fussing over the newest addition to his skin. I could tell he regrets doing it, but it's far too late for regret. The *Ohio State* logo covered most of his upper bicep. I couldn't help but snort at his impulsivity.

He hasn't even been accepted yet.

I chuckle at the thought of him getting into another college and having to hide it for four years. He got it to impress a girl he'd just met and never even got her number.

The beach was the most overcrowded I've ever seen it. The blazing midday sun shone down on us with retribution. It's the hottest day

158

of the summer and it doesn't feel as if it's going to ease up soon. I wipe the perspiration from my brow as Connor rolls down his sleeve to hide the covered-up ink.

"You can't pretend it's not there."

He gnaws on his bottom lip, not even glancing at me.

"I can until I know for certain I've been accepted."

My face falls as his head drops and his shoulders sink. He'd had his heart set on *Ohio State* for as long as I can remember. He'd worked his ass off with hockey and kept his grades up.

Connor has a reputation for being reckless, but when he cares about something, he gives everything he has. I've met no one more dedicated.

"You're going to get in," I said. "Don't stress yourself out and focus on having an epic senior year."

"How can you be so certain?"

"If I could get into college, then anyone can."

My words seemed to reignite his confidence. He squares his shoulders before shoving me.

"You're right." He said. "I have no idea how you got accepted."

The further we walk, the more my feet sink into the sand. Squabbling seagulls flew above our heads and onto the sand. They fought over the dispersed fries and popcorn. I investigated the sea, squinting my eyes at the sunrays poking my eyeballs.

"There's Marcus."

He was lounging on the deck chair with his arms behind his head. His sunglasses were so huge they covered most of his face. I snorted at how ridiculous he looked.

That's what he gets for letting his girlfriend dress him.

I snuck up behind him and pushed him off. He fell face-first into the sand. Connor burst into laughter as I made myself comfortable in the chair.

"You're an asshole." Marcus said, but he couldn't wipe the amused smile off.

"Where's the dementor?"

He rolls his eyes.

"I've told you to stop calling her that."

I raise my hands in defense before glancing at Connor. He gripped his shirt between his fingers, attempting to fan himself. I chuckled before lifting my shirt from my torso and tossed it on the sand.

"Did you seriously get another tattoo?"

I glance at my chest, at the tattoo covered in protective film. My gaze falls on Connor, who is pretending to be admiring the ocean.

"I'm not the only one." Marcus' brows furrow as his eyes dart between me and Connor. "Why don't you take your shirt off, Connie?"

I don't know if it was me outing him or addressing him by the embarrassing nickname that pissed him off the most. He folds his arms across his chest with a pout.

"No thanks," He said. "I'm cold."

"It's the hottest day of the summer."

He scrunches his nose before pulling his shirt over his head. The striking red and black calls our eyes toward his bicep.

"Connor, you haven't even been accepted."

"I know that!" He places his hand on his forehead. "I wasn't thinking!"

I look at Marcus to find him already looking at me before we burst into laughter, not stopping even when our oxygen is depleted. Connor may be an impulsive dumbass, but he never fails in brightening the mood.

12

Olivia

I don't know if it's my loved-up mind, but the sky seems to be an even more magnificent blue today. The birds' song is more melodic, as if they're serenading me with their vibrant orchestra. As if the world had become Utopia before my very eyes.

I straightened out my outfit for the umpteenth time and assessed my appearance, fixing any tattered hairs. Wyatt will be here any second. The thought delivers a hyperactive swarm of butterflies to run rampant inside my gut. I take a deep breath before prancing down the stairs.

As if we'd timed it. The doorbell rings the moment I reach the last step. I failed at remaining casual as I opened the door with an ear-splitting grin.

"Hey." He said before revealing a bouquet of roses from behind his back.

My heart beats against my chest as I take them out of his hand. The floral scent invades my nostrils. I sigh in bliss.

"Thank you."

I stepped aside and motioned him to enter. He follows me into the kitchen and leans against the counter as I scuffle around in search of a vase.

"Who is this?"

Penelope's voice floods the room. Marcus hovers in the doorway.

"I'm Wyatt."

He reaches to shake her hand. Her eyes widened.

"I've been wanting to meet you." She said. "I've heard lots about you!"

I wanted to jump over the counter and seal her mouth shut. She better not say anything else to embarrass me.

"Hopefully not from Reed." Wyatt jokes.

She rolls her eyes.

"No one cares what he has to say, anyway."

Her words put him at ease as the corner of his lip twitched. He's delighted to meet someone who shares his dislike for Reed. I know they'll bond over it.

"We better get going," Marcus said, always quick to defend his best friend. "We've got lots planned."

He barely acknowledges Wyatt as he stalks away from the kitchen. Penelope smiles before trailing after him. I shiver at the icy reception.

"So, are you ready to go?"

I nod, wanting to forget the awkward moment, and place the vase on the counter. He intertwined his fingers with mine before exiting. I smiled the entire way to his car.

It's as if my heart is about to combust.

"Where are we going?"

We'd been in the car for what feels like hours already and it doesn't seem we're stopping soon. However, I've always been impatient.

"It's a surprise."

I roll my eyes despite the escaping grin. I've always detested surprises, but I'm willing to let it slide this time. For him.

We arrived at the Marina, and I furrow my brows as I spot the hordes of ships swaying side to side in perfect harmony.

"What do you think?"

"About what?"

He points to a white and pale blue ship. It's only then I notice *St. James* painted in bold on the side. How did I miss that?

"It looks even better inside."

He grips my hand, dragging me to the boat.

I don't think I've ever been inside a boat, not even *next* to one. I'm giddy as we climb aboard, my eyes darting around a mile a minute. It's an overload of sights and scents. A table overspread with an array of food piqued my attention.

He's put a lot of thought into this.

"Wow."

That's all I could manage.

"Do you like it?"

"What's not to like?"

He seems pleased by my answer as his grin widens and his tense shoulders loosen. He places his hand on my back and leads me to the table to sit. My eyes are as big as the table. *So much indecision.* I gnaw on my bottom lip, hoping he can't hear the excessive rumbling of my stomach.

"So, I've been thinking of hosting a charity hockey match." He said as I reached for the bowl of grapes. "Do you think your brothers and Reed would be interested?"

I freeze. *My brothers? Definitely. Reed? Not so much.*

I gaze at his face, as he seems overjoyed by this project. Who am I to destroy it?

"They'd love to."

I ignore the protests in my mind. Guilt falls into my stomach like quick-drying cement, but it's all worth it to see the beauty of his radiant and sparkling smile. *I would deal with the consequences later.*

Reed

It's safe to say I lost Connor. One moment he was skipping alongside me, blabbering about the *tattoo girl,* followed by dead silence. He has a habit of disappearing. I've found it best to never question his whereabouts.

I needed to clear my head. The ocean was calling me with its siren song. I dawdle along the shore as the water washes around my ankles. A group of kids screamed as I bolted into the freezing water. *Their wails are mind-numbing.* I hurry past them before their banshee calls melt my brain. The sun's rays seep into my skin despite my quickened pace. I cup my hand above my eyes as I hear the distinct call of my name.

I spot Marcus flailing his arms a few feet away. Penelope is lounging on a chair beside him. *Just great.* I feign excitement as I approach them.

"What are you doing here?" He asked, once I reached them.

"Felt like taking a walk."

"Where's Connor?" Penelope asked.

Probably having a better time than me right now.

"I have no clue."

Her phone beeps and she gasps. She places her hand over her mouth, but her smile is too wide to cover up.

"What's got you smiling like that?" Marcus asked.

"Olivia sent a picture. Wyatt took her out on a yacht." She said, before extending the phone out to us.

Marcus gripped the phone for a further inspection, and I looked over his shoulder. It's a bunch of pictures ranging from the gorgeous abyss of the ocean to selfies of her on the edge with Wyatt's arm around her shoulder with matching wide grins.

The latter has me fuming.

It's like a brutal car crash is in my sight, but I cannot seem to tear my eyes away. My jaw clenched so tight that it might shatter into pieces soon. Marcus hands the phone back.

"Not sure how I feel about that." He voices my thoughts.

"She's happy. Be happy for her." Penelope said.

"I wish she'd be happier with someone else."

Even under her sunglasses, I could see her roll her eyes.

What is her deal?

I don't want to hear any more about Wyatt and Olivia, or how perfect they are together, or how happy he makes her. I'm done pretending and lying to myself. I make up a random excuse about needing to get something I left at the house and speed walk away from them and their repetitive conversation. However, another obstacle impedes my solitude.

"Hey, Reed."

Alyssa slides in front of me. Her micro bikini leaves nothing for the imagination, and as much as I hate to admit it, it turns me on. Her unwavering confidence is alluring.

"Hey."

"Where are you going?"

I focused my eyes on her glossed lips.

"To the beach house," I said. "Think I had too much sun."

She pouts.

"That's a shame." She said. "I thought we could hang out."

I'm slow in registering her words as she twirls the ends of her hair.

"You could come with me," I said. "No one else is home."

The pout slides up into a wicked grin as if I fell into her trap.

"I was hoping you'd ask."

I tried to remain unbothered, but the obvious tent trying to break out of my swim trunks gave it away. I doubt she's complaining, though. The moment we enter through the front door, she grabs my wrist and drags me to my bedroom. She shoves me against the door as I succumb to her newfound dominance. My shirt ripped open before I could even register the buttons rolling to the ground.

"Seems like someone had a busy day."

She gestures to my new tattoo covered by plastic.

I can only nod. I don't want to talk. All I want is her plump lips wrapped around me. As if she can sense my thoughts, she drags me towards the bed, shoving me onto my back. The bed squeaks under my weight.

"I left something behind when I was last here." She said. "I was hoping I'd be back."

She ducks under my bed, and I prop myself on my elbows as I become impatient. My eyes widen as she reveals a set of handcuffs.

That was under my bed the entire time?

She crawls onto the bed and straddles me before dangling the handcuffs in my face. Her eyes darken with lust, and I know mine look the same.

"Lay back and enjoy this, baby." She whispers into my ear.

My corner lip rises as I make myself comfortable against the stack of pillows. She reaches over me to cuff my hands to the headboard and I don't resist. I wince at the cold metal, but a shiver of excitement runs down my spine.

As she brushes her lips against my neck, I reach for her, forgetting my hands are restricted. She litters my neck in kisses trailing down. I clench my stomach as her mouth ventures south. I lift my hips as she pulls my pants down. She reaches for my penis. I hissed as she brushed her lips against my sensitive tip and groaned as I was enveloped by her warm mouth. Her skillful tongue worked its magic. I grip her hair, losing all inhibition, and I release a guttural groan.

"Olivia."

The moment the name slips from my tongue, she stops what she's doing. Her eyes connected with mine as if a match had lit them.

Did I just moan Olivia's name?

"What did you just call me?"

I do not know how to get out of this. All I know is that Olivia had slipped into my mind and her name spilled out before I could stop it.

Her scorching glare was as fiery as the pits of hell. She raises her hand and before I can register, my cheek burns. As if she were trying to slap me to hell herself. I couldn't even soothe the burn because of these fucking handcuffs.

"You're a fucking asshole, Reed Adler."

If I had a dollar every time I heard that.

She launches herself off the bed and turns to me with folded arms.

"Don't talk to me ever again."

Before I could get a word in, she bolted out of the room, leaving me cuffed to the bedpost.

13

Olivia

To say it was the greatest day of my life would be an understatement. After the phenomenal seaside experience, he walked me to my door and sealed it off with a stomach-fluttering kiss. The moment I walked into the beach house; I noticed it was uncharacteristically quiet.

Where is everybody?

I trudge through the downstairs area of the house before slowly venturing upstairs. I strain my ears for any sound of life, and I pick up on the distinct sound of rattling. With furrowed brows, I venture further down the hallway.

It's coming from Reed's bedroom.

I notice his door is wide open, so I risk a peek inside... only to burst into a fit of laughter. My stomach aches as I hunch over. My legs almost gave out.

Reed is handcuffed to the bedpost, staring at me like a deer in headlights. He's covered by the bed sheets, but I can only imagine he's completely nude.

"What happened?" I asked once my laughter died down.

"Alyssa." He said, followed by a sigh. "At least I know I'm not into handcuffs."

I roll my eyes, trying not to smile, but I can't help it. Only Reed would find himself in this predicament.

"Are you going to help me out of this or not?"

I folded my arms across my chest and placed my finger on my chin as if contemplating a conflicting decision.

"I will," I said and reached into my back pocket. "After I take a few pictures."

I giggle as I take a horde of pictures. The perfect blackmail. The photographic evidence is indisputable.

"Stop."

Once I'm satisfied with the images, I set off to search for the keys.

"Try looking underneath the underwear." He said. "She was in such a rush she left them behind."

My face contorted in disgust as I lifted a lacy thong with the tip of my fingers. The key sparkles on the ground. I dangle it, but do not free him.

"What now?"

"A part of me wants to leave you like this and have the others make fun of you," I said. "But if they do, I won't have anything to hold against you."

With that in mind, I slot the key into the locks. The second both hands are freed, he rubs his wrists. He must have been there for a while.

"What did you do to piss her off?"

179

He halts his movements.

"Why do you assume I did something?"

"She wouldn't leave you tied to the bedpost for nothing."

He shrugs.

"Maybe she's just into bondage."

I roll my eyes but decide not to question him further. He reaches for the sheets, ready to yank them off.

"Wait!" I said. "Let me leave the room first."

His corner lip rises.

"It's not like you haven't seen it before."

I roll my eyes at his cockiness. He tosses the sheet off him and I look away in time. I cover my eyes with my hands.

"What is wrong with you?"

"A bunch of stuff." He said. "You used to love it when I did this."

I turn my back to him and inhale in frustration.

"That's all in the past now."

I direct one more hateful look before storming out of the room.

I'd spent the rest of the day thinking of how to bring up Wyatt's charity match. I couldn't just drop it on him. I have to butter him up first. Which is why I made lasagna. His all-time favorite meal.

Reed hasn't left his room since our awkward interaction, and I couldn't have been more grateful. I couldn't deal with being around him for a second longer. Especially alone.

I heard the front door opening, followed by the commotion of Connor's booming voice. They all shuffle into the kitchen, and Connor rushes to my side.

"I'm starving!" He yelled.

He reaches his finger out for a taste, but I swat it away just in time. He holds his hand to his chest with a pout. I ignore him and turn to Marcus. His eyes are set on me with an imploring gaze. As if he's on to me. I remain stoic and offer him a friendly smile.

"Lasagna?" I asked.

"What do you want from me?"

I hate how he knows me.

I tilted my head to the side and scratched my cheek. My mouth opens and closes like a goldfish.

"What do you mean?" I asked. "I got home early and thought you'd be hungry."

He folds his arms across his chest and raises his brow. As if he's saying, *do you really think I'm that naïve?*

"Want to try that again?"

I sigh and drop my shoulders.

"Wyatt is hosting a charity hockey match, and he was hoping you'd both play."

I gesture to Marcus and Connor. They glance at each other as if they were having an extrasensory conversation. It involved some strange contortions of the face and eyes. I can tell they're messing with me. Connor grins.

"Give me a slice of lasagna and you have a deal."

I knew Connor would be easy to convince. I just never expected Marcus to be such a challenge. And if Marcus is so tough to crack, then Reed will be near impossible. Just as I'm about to accept defeat, Penelope, forever my guardian angel, gives Marcus a nudge.

"Come on, babe, it's for charity." She said with her deep, impactful pout that would make a seven-year-old cave in.

"Fine."

I raise my hand in celebration and wrap my arms around his neck.

"Thank you. Thank you. Thank you." I said before reaching over to Penelope for a victorious high-five.

I slump against the counter, feeling satisfied that I'd won over two-thirds.

I'll take that as a victory.

"Please tell me there's lasagna."

I hear *his* voice before he enters.

"Sure is," Marcus said. "It comes with a price, though."

Reed halts.

"What?"

Marcus turns his attention to me as he telepathically tells me to ask the dreaded question. I take a dramatic inhale before plastering on my sweetest smile.

"Wyatt is hosting a charity hockey match, and he'd love to have you guys take part."

The room was like a vacuum, sucking up any hint of noise. It became so silent I could hear myself gulp in fear of the imminent outburst.

"Sounds like fun."

I choke on my saliva. *Did he just say that?*

"What?" I sputter.

"I said it sounds like fun," He said, peering at me as if I'd just grown an extra head. "Can I have some lasagna now?"

I move to the side, still trying to comprehend how effortless it all was. *Too effortless.* He'd agreed immediately, not even with one snarky comment. Was this his way of keeping me happy? So I wouldn't reveal how he'd been tied to the bed for hours by his kinky *friend with benefits?*

It's the only logical explanation.

It's best to not fight and accept that everything has worked out the way I hoped with less effort than I thought.

Reed

I glare at my ceiling as my phone buzzes beside me. *Alyssa.* I'm hoping the battery would just die but I charged it this morning. I rub my eyes until I see stars as the vibrations from my phone pierce my skull. I groan before pressing *decline* for the umpteenth time. I thought she never wanted to talk to me again.

The knock on my door gives me a new sense of purpose. A welcomed distraction from the nuisance.

"Come in!"

I expected it to be Marcus or Connor. Even Penelope was a more likely choice. I didn't expect Olivia to be hovering in the doorway.

"Was I interrupting something?"

I shake my head. The ambivalence is giving me a migraine. I'm not sure if I'm thankful for the distraction or dreading this interaction. She steps into my room but still hovers near the door as if she's ready to make a break for it. She twirls her fingers as she sways back and forth on the heels of her feet. I knew that look all too well.

"Whatever you need to ask me, ask away."

"Why did you agree so effortlessly?"

"Did you not want me to?"

She weaves her fingers through her hair.

"That's not what I mean." She said. "I just didn't expect you to agree that fast."

"You said it's for charity." I shrugged before my corner lip stumbled into a grin. "And I get to kick Wyatt St. James' ass."

She rolls her eyes and folds her arms.

"I should have known that would be the reason."

I tuck my arms behind my head.

"It seems like a win-win to me."

She says nothing, but her eyes reflect her thoughts. *Her rage.*

Is it bad that it's turning me on?

"Well, that's all I wanted to know."

She turns to leave, but I call her name.

"My bedroom is always open for you, Olive." I grinned as her fists tightened at her sides. "Day or night."

Her shoulders stiffen, but she never once turns to look at me. I watch in amusement as she marches out of my room, her stomps echoing through the hallway, followed by the slam of her door. I grin in satisfaction before tilting my head back and closing my eyes, falling into blissful unconsciousness despite the incessant buzzing of my phone.

I woke up to the glowing yellow light of the moon as the ethereal glow consumed my bedroom. I glanced out my window at the picturesque navy backdrop for the full moon.

There were no stars to steal the spotlight, making every crater visible.

I must have slept longer than intended.

I stretch my back, groaning in delight at the satisfying feeling of my muscles stretching. They were stiff from my awkward sleeping position. I trudge downstairs to find Marcus and Penelope eating each other's faces in the kitchen.

"People eat here."

They pull away.

"Someone had a bad nap." Penelope said.

"For your information, the nap was amazing," I said. "It's the nightmare that I just walked into that made me cranky."

She rolls her eyes and clings tighter onto Marcus, if that is even possible. She's always been skilled at annoying me.

"What's the plan for tonight?" Marcus asked.

"Well, where is everyone else?"

The house is far too silent.

"Connor is at another party. Chelsea went out with a new friend she made and Olivia left with Wyatt about an hour ago."

Of course she did.

"Well, I will not be your third wheel."

My shoulders slump. Despite my lengthy nap, I still feel myself drowning in exhaustion. However, this feels more mental than physical.

"I'm so happy you said that." Penelope said. "We're having a date night."

I tilt my upper lip in disgust, but Marcus seems to find my reaction humorous. I hover around until they bid their goodbyes, leaving me to sulk in the intolerable silence.

I scroll through *Instagram* as I like a few posts of people from college, some of them with their friends, families, and significant others. I couldn't help but snort at one of Connor's posts. He's standing in his kitten swim trunks with his arms around some friends.

He's never boring.

I scroll more until a specific post catches my eye. Olivia posted it a few minutes ago. I glare at the image of her smiling face with her arms wrapped around that douchebag's neck. His arm was around her waist. The breathtaking ocean backdrop amplifies the romance. I grit my teeth at the heart-shaped caption.

I lock my phone and toss it on the counter. There's an unpleasant taste in my mouth like rising bile.

I wanted to chop his arm off.

My hair falls in front of my eyes, and I brush it back in frustration. My hands shake. I've always been bad at controlling my anger, especially with Wyatt St. James.

I can still see the image in my mind.

I reach for my phone and charge out of the desolate home. My legs knew where I was going, and my mind knew it, too. I must have left a distinct trail of footsteps in the sand as I stomped my feet along the shore. I could only imagine how I must look at onlookers. Stomping my feet like a scolded toddler.

I'm pathetic.

I debated turning around, going back home, and calling it a night. It would be the wise thing to do. The responsible thing.

Too bad I'm neither of those things.

My impulsiveness clouded my judgment as I spotted Olivia with that douchebag. They stood close together, as she seemed to be engaged in a discussion with one of his douchebag friends. I marched towards them as the rage took over my thoughts, but a recognizable voice halted my rampaging strut.

"It's not a good idea to do that."

I squint my eyes as the moon assists in the lighting. I step closer and spot Brynlee sitting on the sand with her arms locked around her knees as if she's bracing herself against the chilled breeze. Or something else.

"Do what?"

"Cause trouble."

I furrow my brows and fold my arms across my chest.

"I have no idea what you're talking about."

She chuckles.

"You were intent on sabotage."

I feign ignorance. She will not be the know-it-all guru this time.

"I have no idea what you're talking about."

She raises her left brow and tilts her head as if to say, *really?* I shrug.

"You seem to forget you've filled me in on your history." She said. "Word of advice. If you're trying to win her back, this isn't the way to do it."

I gaze out toward the sickening view of him whispering in her ear before she breaks out into laughter. My shoulders slump.

"I hate that you're right," I said to Brynlee as I sat down beside her. "She looks happy."

She shrugs as she gazes in their direction.

"I believe there's varying degrees of happiness."

"What does that even mean?"

She doesn't tear her gaze from the sickening scene.

"You could be happy with someone, but that doesn't mean you couldn't be *happier* with someone else."

I drop my head, brushing my fingers along the sand, and think of all the heartbreak I've put her through.

"I'm no good for her," I said. "She's been through so much anger and heartbreak because of me."

Brynlee placed a comforting hand on my shoulder, but I couldn't look her in the eye.

"Love is a risk. You could never break someone's heart if you never had it." She said. "True love is always worth mending."

I scowl at the calming seas as they contradict my thoughts.

"No one said anything about true love."

She scoffs and bumps my shoulder with hers.

"I've seen the way you look at her." She said. "You do little to hide it."

My face contorted as I gazed up at the darkened sky.

"I spent almost a year trying to deny it, but this summer brought back too many memories," I said. "I never stopped loving her. It was just easier to pretend when I was at college, and she wasn't around."

She places a comforting hand on my shoulder.

"Chin up, buddy." She said with a grin. "I know you'll find each other again."

14

Olivia

Today is the day of the charity hockey match. I shouldn't have been so nervous, but I can't help it. I can't help but fear Reed is going to do something reckless and ruin the entire day. This is all meant to help others. It's not for his vendetta against Wyatt and their fatuous rivalry.

Locals and vacationers alike filled the rink to the brim. Everyone is eager to bear witness to this debut.

I'm the opposite.

I'm attempting to remain neutral because I have individuals I care about on both teams. The only thing calming me down is the thought that this is only fun and games. There should be no animosity or competitiveness.

I arrived at the rink a few hours before everyone else, insisting on helping Wyatt set up.

"Which charity is your team supporting?" I question Wyatt as I stack the abundance of flyers on the entrance table.

"Dementia research." He said as his smile dropped a bit. "My gran has it."

I smiled at his answer. Despite the circumstances, it's sweet he's supporting a charity close to his heart.

We arrange everything in silence until he clears his throat. I turned to him to find him scratching the nape of his neck.

"I wanted to ask you something." He walked to his backpack. He unveils a shirt and, from further inspection, it's one of his hockey jerseys. *St. James* is as clear as day on the back. My eyes widen as he places it in my hands. "Would you wear my jersey today?"

I gaze at the fabric as if it were a snake. I don't know what I was expecting, but it wasn't this. My cheeks felt as if I set them alight.

"I'd love to."

I saw his shoulders slumped as if he was nervous about my answer, but my positive feedback was the relief he needed. His grin is like the highest reward as I wear the oversized garment. His inebriating aroma is like an addiction. I couldn't get enough.

"You look amazing." He said. "It gives me motivation to play better so I can make wearing it worthwhile."

My cheeks feel puffy and hot, as if a nest of hornets had stung me. They burn even more at the thought of how ridiculous I must look. I wanted to reply with something witty, but it felt as if my heart was beating so fast it took off and got lodged in my throat.

I could feel our lips inching closer like a magnetic pull. His bottom lip brushed mine before someone calling his name broke us apart.

I frowned as one of his teammates motioned him over. He glanced at me.

"I'll see you later," I said, to mask my disappointment. "Good luck."

He leans down and places a chaste kiss on my cheek. My stomach somersaults.

"That's what you're here for." He said, before rushing off to join his team, leaving me a flustered mess.

Reed

Screw Wyatt St. James. He doesn't give a shit about charity. He only cares about his image. This is all an excuse to make himself look good.

I tie my laces as he charms a few of the locals. He shakes hands with them and ruffles the hair of the children. I can't help but scoff.

It's like he's running for mayor or something.

I wanted to wipe that shit-eating grin from his face. I imagine hitting him in the jaw and taking pleasure in it until I draw blood. I was cursing him under my breath as Marcus skated towards me.

"What's your deal?"

He squeezes onto the bench with me to tie his own laces.

"Nothing."

I don't remove my heated gaze from the spectacle. He snorts.

"Let's just pretend I haven't known you your entire life."

I make no acknowledgment of his words, not in the mood for one of his characteristic motivational talks. I wanted to wallow in self-pity and drown in my flooding hatred for the *douche* a few feet away. Marcus could never resist being the angel to chase my demons away.

"Don't let your temper get the best of you," he said. "Remember, this is for charity."

I nod my head and glance at my clasped hands.

"Too bad. I can never resist a chance to bruise his ego a little."

No matter how hard he tries to fight it, a minuscule smile appears.

"I suppose a minor bruise couldn't hurt," he said before patting my back. "I'll meet you out there."

He steps onto the ice and skates toward Connor. I take a moment to compose myself before stepping onto the ice, remaining motionless as I take in my surroundings. I feel all the tension draining as I'm consumed in my element. The adoring crowd. The sound of the skates slicing through the ice.

My eyes land on Olivia, leaning on the barrier to get a closer look at the action. The moment I rake in her appearance, the peace gets sucked into the black hole of rage. The shirt adorning her body was all too familiar. I couldn't look away. I could recognize it from a mile away.

It's *his*.

I skate toward her with my jaw clenched to the point it feels like it is going to snap.

"Why would you wear his jersey when your brothers are playing?" I asked the moment I was in earshot.

She folds her arms across her chest and juts out her hip, her cheerful demeanor souring.

"I want to."

Her attitude is like gasoline to the flame. I can hear Marcus' voice telling me to remain calm - forever my angel. However, the darkness casts out his light.

"Take it off."

"No."

I bite my lip until I taste blood. Her smug grin ignites the flames.

"Take it off *now*, Olivia."

"Calm down, Reed. It's a charity match. Not the NHL."

I clench my fists at my side.

"I won't ask again."

"I said *no*."

I square my shoulders and take a deep breath, exhaling my frustration, before looking her square in the eyes with a sinister smirk.

"Fine," I said. "Don't get mad at me when they cart your boyfriend out on a stretcher."

Her jaw drops as I skate backward. I send a condescending wave before turning around to join the rest of my team. The spectators have doubled in size as if there's nothing better to do.

I guess the whole charity thing drew them in.

I glanced towards Wyatt's side, and it was as if I'd forgotten why we were playing. I kept having flashbacks to championships and our unquenchable rivalry. Despite everything, I had to beat him.

The moment the match began, I treated it like a championship final. I was doing it for charity, but now it's become so much more than that. Seeing her wearing his jersey, as if he was trying to mark his territory, has ignited my rage.

He's taken it too far.

The moment one of his teammates passes the puck to him, I charge for him. I ram my shoulder into him, catching him unawares. He crashes to the ice, and the crowd *oohs*. I place my hands in the air, pretending it was an accident. I can feel his hateful gaze piercing the side of my head, but I barely acknowledge him. His teammates help him up as I reach Marcus and Connor.

"What was that about?" Connor asked.

I shrug.

"The guy can't take a hit."

He snorts.

"Well, let's play it safe for now." Marcus said.

Connor rolls his eyes.

"That seems less fun," he said, before nudging my shoulder. "He always has to be the fun sponge."

Marcus raises his hands.

"You bruised his ego. I thought that's what you wanted."

I glance at him from across the rink to find him staring at me already. Even from a distance, I can sense the intensity, the rage. I can't help but smirk in his direction and send him a playful wave with my fingers. He gripped his stick so tight that if he had any strength, he would have broken it in half.

The game resumed as Marcus stole the puck from the opposition. He shot it at me. I line up to take the shot until I'm knocked to the ground. I watch as the puck and my stick glide away from me, leaving me burning with so much rage it feels as if the ice is going to melt from under me. Wyatt towers over me, glancing down in satisfaction. *That triggered me.*

Lifting myself off the ice, I charge toward him and tackle him to the ground with a *WWE* main event-worthy *spear.* I don't know when the gloves and helmets came off, but I only realized once my bare fist collided with his jaw. I ignored my split knuckles and continued with my onslaught of hits, not stopping until someone's arms encircled my waist and they hoisted me from his battered body. I struggle to escape their locked grip.

It could only be Marcus.

I confirmed my suspicions as his demanding voice booms over the ruckus.

"That's enough, Reed, let it go."

He's one of the few people I'd never dare argue with. I let him drag me away from the prying eyes and into the locker room. He makes me sit in the corner seat, like a kid in time out, and points an accusatory finger at me.

"Do not leave this seat." he said before leaving me to spew in my rage.

I couldn't help but overthink the ways I wanted to murder him. To humiliate him. I wanted to pretend that it was all because of a ridiculous sports rivalry, but I know my disdain for him is more than just on the surface. I let my emotions get the best of me. My *jealousy* got the best of me.

15

Olivia

I've never considered murder. Until now. *A Million Ways to Murder Reed Adler* sounds like a future bestseller to me. They'd make *Netflix* documentaries about it.

I watched the entire fight like a useless bystander. I'd only released my bated breath when Marcus hauled Reed away. Wyatt's team helped him to his feet and led him to the bench. I rushed through the crowd and pressed myself against the tempered glass, hoping to get his attention. I flail my arms until he looks my way.

Are you okay? I mouth to him.

He glances down at his skates, shakes his head, and lifts himself from the bench before bolting into the locker room. I don't take my gaze off his retreating figure until he's out of sight. My eyes brim with tears, not out of sadness but of anger.

This is all Reed's fault.

If he could have halted his immaturity for one charity match, then none of this would have happened. Wyatt wouldn't be hurt, and we wouldn't be two players down. I wanted to find him, wrap my arms around his neck, and smother him, but I couldn't. I needed to stay and watch my brothers play. They're playing for a charity close to my heart and I wanted to see this through. They both know how much it means to me and it melts my heart that it's the charity they chose. I couldn't leave now. However, the moment this match ends, I am going to destroy Reed Adler.

The crowd was still buzzing from the great game as they flocked out of the arena. I stayed put, waiting for Marcus or Connor to approach. I beamed with pride as they spoke to a few of the locals and shook a few hands. Connor's smile was so wide it looked like his face would crack. My brothers have always loved hockey, but for Connor, it was a deeper level of devotion.

He wouldn't give up hockey for anything in the world.

They stepped off the ice, and I ran towards them, not even giving them a moment to take off their skates. I spread my arms wide and embraced them both.

"You both were amazing!" I said. "I almost cried when I saw the charity you chose."

"It's no big deal," Marcus said. He's always been too humble. "Reed chose the charity."

I pinched a nerve in my neck at the sudden whiplash I got. My eyes feel as if they're going to pop out of their sockets.

"You're kidding."

"No, he said he'd only play if he got to pick the charity."

I didn't know how to react to this. Why would he choose it? Why would he care? *Don't forget what he did.* The voice in the back of my mind reminds me, and it brings my rage back to the surface.

"I'm going back to the house," I said. "See you later."

The entire walk home, I spew in my resentment. Reed could have ruined something so amazing for me. I'd been waiting for ages for a guy like Wyatt to stumble into my life, and I might have lost him before anything else could have developed. All because Reed Adler always has to insert himself where he doesn't belong. The moment I stepped into our home, and was greeted with silence, I felt my brain running a marathon. I stormed to my room, but Reed's open door made me halt. I peer inside. He's not here.

I'm overtaken by the irrational devil on my shoulder telling me to make him hurt the way he did me. With that in mind, I charge into his room and grab a pile of his clothes out of his drawer. I approach the open window and toss it out without hesitation, watching as it sashays with the slight breeze before littering the driveway. I felt empowered and tossed more out the window. Whoever arrives home will think I've lost my mind.

Maybe I have.

"What the *fuck?*" Reed yells from outside.

I rush to the window with a satisfied grin.

"That's what you get for being an asshole!"

"What did I do?"

He tosses his arms up before dropping them at his sides. For a moment, I think he's joking, but he looks clueless. As if he's so naïve to his own faults.

"Are you so self-absorbed that you forgot what you did to Wyatt?"

He scratches the back of his neck.

"Yeah."

I know he was doing this to piss me off. It's working. Blinded by rage, I grab the nearest object to toss out. It's his lucky hockey stick. The first stick he ever got.

"Olivia, *no.*"

"Give me a reason I shouldn't toss this out."

Despite our distance, I could feel the sharp daggers in his eyes grazing my skin.

"Toss that stick out the window, and Mr. Cuddles is taking a swim with the fishes."

He knows how much that stuffed bear means to me. As much as this tasteless stick means to him.

"You wouldn't dare."

"Try me."

I sigh in defeat and return the stick to its rightful position, returning to the window, but he's nowhere in sight. I lean further out to glimpse at him, but he's disappeared.

I give up my search and move away from my window. My scream halts in my throat as his figure looms in the doorway. He folded his arms across his chest as he leaned against the doorway with a lazy smirk.

"You know, I have the right mind to taser you."

"If that's what helps you to get off," he said, stepping into his room. "Who am I to stop you?"

With every step he takes forward, I take backward. We continue the charade until I'm flush against the wall as if I were part of the wallpaper. My throat closes as he moves closer, so close his breath hits my face.

It's been so long since I've been so close to Reed.

Last summer felt like another lifetime. His fingers brush along my arm and I do nothing to stop it. His touch is nostalgic. My brain is yelling at me to shake it off and to create as much distance from him as possible, but my body refuses to follow orders. He tucks a strand of my chestnut locks behind my ear, but his hand remains against my cheek, sharing his warmth. His crystal eyes look into mine with such an intensity I can't help but avert my gaze.

"Do I make you nervous, Olive?" he asked. I always hated that dreaded nickname. "After all this time?"

"You don't," I said. "You make me uncomfortable."

He snorts.

"We both know that's not the truth." he said, inching closer. My breath hitches. "Tell me to move and I will."

His bottom lip brushes against mine. I'd forgotten how a subtle touch from him could rile me up. My attempts at remaining stoic were feeble. My entire body became littered with goosebumps. His lips brush against my ear.

"You don't need to fight it. I feel the same way." He moves his head back with an intoxicating smirk. "I can't resist you anymore, either."

His confession takes me by surprise, but not as much as his lips connecting to mine. I freeze, unable to decipher my emotions through the flurry of ambivalent thoughts.

Had I spent so long distancing myself from Reed because of his unforgivable actions? Or is it because I knew I wouldn't be able to resist his charismatic charm? There was always something about him that could pull me back in, no matter how much I tried to fight it.

He's beguiling.

I'd spent the entire time deliberating on my thoughts, that I'd never thought to kiss him back. He pulled away with a look of defeat, a look I'd never seen on Reed's face before. It's as if he'd planned this entire thing in his head and it backfired. He pushed himself from the wall, but I stopped him before my brain could warn me.

I gripped the back of his head and pulled him back in. I attached our lips with an underlying urgency as if it were life or death. It seemed I wouldn't be able to take another breath without his lips on mine. He doesn't take long to raise the intensity, pressing me between the wall and his body. I held back my moans, even when he dug his fingers into my exposed hips, but they slid past my lips the moment his lips moved to my neck.

My sweet spot.

"We shouldn't be doing this."

My conscience speaks for me, but I do nothing to stop our intimate exchange.

"Please stop talking."

My breath hitches in my throat as he trails his fingers down the back of my thighs. I gasp as he hauls me up and wraps my legs around his waist, flinching at the momentary coldness of the wall as he uses it for support, but his urgent kisses warm me up. I grip the back of his hair, feeling a sense of satisfaction as it elicits a moan from him. Our oxygen supply runs short and our hasty breaths mix as he places his forehead against mine. His electric eyes pierce into mine.

Neither of us speaks as his left hand trails up between my legs. I suck in my stomach as he traces over it, gasping as his impalpable movement brushes over my breast. His hand slides along my collarbone before cupping the side of my neck.

"I knew you wanted this as much as I do." He whispers as our lips brush.

I should have pushed him off and slapped him in the face for even attempting to kiss me after everything. My mind was telling me to escape this emotional hold he had on me, yet I couldn't resist the feelings fluttering through me.

His lips are like heaven and hell.

I lean in to attach our lips together again, but he moves his head back with an infuriating grin.

"Say you want me," he said. "Do it, baby."

His grin never falters.

"What?"

"Say. You. Want. Me." he said. "Say it and I will give you what you want."

My body was scorching, but not from pleasure. I became enraged at how he'd reeled me in and regained the upper hand. My soft gaze hardens.

"No." I said with as much venom as I could muster.

Before I could even blink, he'd set me down and created a sizable distance between us.

"If that's the case," he said. "Then you can't have me."

I watch in enraged disbelief as he walks backward with an arrogant stride, waving *goodbye* with his fingers before leaving me alone in *his* room.

What the fuck did I just get myself in to?

Reed

I regret stopping our moment. I'd waited so long to have her lips against mine again, only to have my darned ego ruin the moment. But I knew it had to be done. I had to have her crave me as much as I do her. I'd left her wanting more, and now I know for certain she reciprocates my desire.

She's just as stubborn as I am.

Ever since our intimate exchange, the thoughts of our future exchanges had enraptured me. My entire persona had shifted as if I were seeing the world through fresh eyes. It had magnified my confidence.

I skip down the steps but stop halfway at the sound of yelling. I strain my ears to find the source of the noise.

Marcus and Penelope.

"I have no idea why we're fighting about this."

Marcus' tone held a hint of urgency and desperation.

"There's no way you're that clueless."

"Well, I am!"

I've known him long enough to pick up on the frustration in his voice.

"Whatever, Marcus. I'm done fighting over this." She said. "I'm done with everything."

My eyes widened at her words. Did she just break up with him? I halt my breath, wondering what's coming, but there's only the sound of footsteps, followed by the slamming of a door. I wait a few minutes before descending the stairs and peering around the wall into the kitchen. Marcus' elbows are on the counter with his head in his hands. He tattered his hair from running his hands through it. A nervous habit.

"Marcus." I announced my presence, but he made no recognition. "What just happened?"

He groans and lifts his head. His face is blotchy and covered in dried-up tears until more fall down like a cycle of misery.

"We broke up."

"Why?"

He sniffs. His faraway gaze is unsettling.

"It's not important." He pushes himself from the counter. "I just need to be alone right now."

I move aside as he marches out of the room and up the stairs. The sound of a door slamming follows. I bite the inside of my cheek as I think of their unpleasant exchange. What could have caused such animosity between them? My stomach clenches as a theory enters my mind. *Is it because of me?* What if my unpleasant exchange with *St. James* annoyed more than just Olivia?

I speed walk out the front door in search of Penelope. She couldn't have gotten far, considering her car was still in the driveway. I wrack my brain for ideas on where she'd go, but I barely know a thing about her.

Perhaps the beach?

It's the ideal place to mull over your thoughts. The soothing waves are perfect for a therapeutic outlet. The journey to the beach is short and I don't waste a second looking for her. I look all around me. The sky was ablaze with the fire of the setting sun as the sand crystals glowed and sparkled underneath my feet. I needed to find her before the night took over.

Why does this beach have to be so big?

I cover my eyes with my hands and squint into the distance. My stomach twists in anxiousness.

There she is.

I kick my feet into the sand and sprint towards her retreating form, yelling her name with every step. She hears my calls and turns around.

"What do you want, Reed?"

For the first time, her words hold no animosity, only pain. My name was always bitter on her tongue, but it was as if she didn't care about my presence. Or anything at all.

"What happened between you and Marcus?"

She retracts as if I'd slapped her.

"*Excuse me?*"

"What did you fight about?"

"I don't think that's any of your business."

She scoffs before turning to leave, but I grip her arm.

"Was it about me?"

She bites her bottom lip and shakes her head.

"What does it matter?" She mumbles and yanks her arm from my grip. "It doesn't matter anymore."

I run around her and block her from walking away.

"It matters," I said. "Why would you argue about me?"

Her tear-stricken eyes dry out from her fiery glare. I almost melted on the spot from the animosity.

"Are you kidding?" She tosses her hands up in the air. "We always argue over you!"

I choke on my saliva. I don't know what I expected her response to be, but it wasn't this.

"What do you mean?"

She shakes her head in disbelief.

"We always fight over how Marcus will always defend *your* selfish actions." She said. "Like today, at the hockey match, *you* were a complete jerk, but he'd always step in to defend *you*, to reassure everyone *you're* not the complete jackass *you* portray yourself to be."

She points an accusatory finger with each emphasis. I never knew it was possible to feel claustrophobic near the ocean, but I've proven that theory to be erroneous.

"He's my best friend. He's going to defend me."

My words were like gasoline to unruly flames.

"I'm sick of it and I'm sick of you always trying to insert yourself into our problems!" She said before another onslaught of tears hit. "You've won."

I get a sinking feeling in my stomach as if I'd swallowed an anchor. My thoughts overcrowded my mind to where I'd hardly registered her walking away.

"Penelope, wait!" I said, catching up with her. "You're making a big mistake."

She twirls around with deranged eyes. I take a step back.

"Why do you even care?"

"Marcus is the greatest person I know. He loves you more than anything in the world." I said. "If you're going to let my dumb ass be the reason you break up, then you're making the biggest mistake of your life."

She opens her mouth, then closes it.

"It won't take another girl long to figure out what a catch he is, and you'll lose him forever." I continue my rant. "He's the guy I wish I could be, but I don't even scratch the surface. Get your guy before someone else does."

She runs her fingers through her strawberry blonde locks as if she's trying to digest my discrepant words.

"Why are you helping me?" She asked. "You hate me."

I chuckled, surprised by my own actions.

"I could never hate someone that makes Marcus the best version of himself."

Her cerulean eyes darted back and forth as if waiting for the prank to reveal. She scans my face for any sign of disingenuity, but I know there's none. *Despite it all, I meant every word I said.*

"Maybe I had you all wrong."

She was speaking to herself, and I didn't want to interrupt. I shrug and tuck my hands into my front pockets.

"If you ever tell anyone about this conversation, I will deny it until death."

The corner of her lip rises.

"I doubt anyone would believe me, anyway."

Our uncharacteristic interaction was too much for me to absorb. I didn't know what to say next. Luckily, she broke the tension.

"I'm going to talk to Marcus."

I nod my head and turn to the scenic setting sun.

"Reed."

I whipped around, surprised Penelope hadn't bolted yet.

"Yeah?"

"Although you can be a complete douchebag, you've always been a good friend to Marcus." She said. "Just want you to know that."

I'm touched by her confession. I couldn't bite off my smile.

"Thank you."

She nods in recognition before strolling back to the beach house. I replay our conversation in my head, knowing that I'd done the right thing. For their entire relationship, I'd made snide remarks about Marcus getting too serious, pleading for him to be single. However, his happiness always came first, and he's never been happier since he met her. *That's what genuine friends do.*

16

Olivia

What have I done? What was I thinking? I wasn't. Reed Adler got under my skin again and reeled me in, only to send me back with the fish. *It's last summer all over again.*

I didn't have any excuse for why I let it happen. I wasn't drunk; I didn't hit my head; I was aware of the situation.

I wanted it to happen.

Its why being around him is so dangerous. There's too much temptation. Despite my insistence, my feelings for him never diminished. They're dormant in the back of my mind, and I'd tried my best to keep them locked away.

Yet, all it took was a kiss to break the seal.

Despite it all, only pain and heartbreak follow Reed Adler. I cannot have history repeat itself. I need to fight the temptation.

A knock on my door whisks my inner conflict away. I hadn't moved from my blanket cave. I didn't even realize the sun was seeping in through my open windows until I lifted my head out from under the sheets.

"Are you planning on getting out of bed soon?"

Marcus halts just inside my room. I shake my head with a sigh.

"I don't think so."

He says nothing, but his footsteps become more distinct. My bed creaks under his weight as he sits on the edge.

"What's going on?"

"Just feeling tired. Got little sleep last night."

It's not a lie. I couldn't sleep with the rampant thoughts running through my mind all night. I relived my interaction with Reed like a nightmare. A nightmare that I can't escape even when awake.

"Are you sure? If you're feeling sick again we can-"

"I'm not sick again, Marcus."

"It wouldn't hurt to make sure."

I know his insistence is coming from a good place, but it was getting far too annoying. Would I ever be able to live last year down? Or will I forever have the dark reminder hovering over my head?

"Marcus, I promise this isn't like last time," I said. "I just didn't sleep well."

He analyzes my face for any hint of dishonesty, but I remain impassive.

"Fine," He said with a sigh. "I'm going to get some ice cream with Penelope. Want to join us?"

I snort.

"I'd rather not be a third wheel," I said. "Thank you, though."

He smiles as he hesitates about whether to leave. However, after a moment's deliberation, he stands up and exits the room. I basked in the silence, but it was short-lived as Chelsea ran into my room. She squealed as she jumped on my bed.

"Chels, what are you doing?"

I toss the sheets over my head, but she yanks them off.

"The better question is, what are *you* doing?" She asked.

She's clutching a bouquet of roses in her hands. How did I not see that before?

"Who gave you flowers?"

I lift myself, but I don't move from the warmth of my sheets.

"Sadly, no one." She said. "These are for you."

She shoves the bouquet in my hand. I furrow my brows.

"You got me flowers?"

"Not me, Wyatt." She said with the widest grin I've ever seen. "Read the card."

I dig around until my hands brush against an envelope. My name is written in cursive, followed by a heart. I haven't spoken to Wyatt since his altercation with Reed. I open the letter.

I'm sorry about how I reacted at the rink. You deserve the ultimate happiness and I hope I can give it.

A wave of regret washes over me as I glance at the breathtaking bouquet. I hadn't thought about him since my kiss with Reed.

How selfish could I be?

I have an amazing guy that buys me flowers and gifts and always takes the time to make me feel special, and I sabotage it by kissing my douchebag of an ex.

And the worst part is I enjoyed doing it.

I didn't think about Wyatt. I behaved impulsively and it shouldn't happen again.

"Are you going to call him?"

I'm not sure.

"Of course I am," I said. "Why wouldn't I?"

A blanket of generous velvet engulfs the sky, illuminating the galaxy above. The stars flutter and shimmer in happiness as if they were mocking me. The gentle breeze danced through my hair in perfect harmony with the poised ocean waves. I couldn't hear much as the tranquil silence became disturbed by the energetic crowds scattering along the shore.

Wyatt's band is playing tonight. He texted me earlier asking if I'd come and watch, but I haven't seen him since I got here. It's understandable he's busy, but it would have been nice to wish him luck before he went on.

I'd lost Chelsea the moment we stepped foot on the beach. The entire way here she'd been talking my ear off about a guy she met a few days ago and they'd met up a few times. I haven't seen her this excited over someone in a long time, so being ditched by her isn't something I'd cry myself to sleep over.

I clutched my drink against my chest as I brushed past the crowd in search of somewhere to sit before the show, but as expected, all the seats were occupied. I glance around the area, hoping to find one, but I make eye contact with a questionable group of guys.

It's wrong to judge a book by its cover, but I would call this an exception. The ringleader of the rowdy bunch chugged the remaining liquid from a bottle of beer before tossing it to the ground, not caring if he'd hit someone. We made eye contact, and I resisted the urge to look away. Instead, I stood my ground, not taking my eyes off him.

"You like what you see, sweetheart?"

I don't say a word. He seems to take offense to my lack of response as launches from the table and speed walks to me, but before he can even take two steps, a figure blocks his way.

"I'd reconsider that if I were you."

Reed towers over the troublesome asshole.

"What are you going to do about it?"

The guy's bravado falters despite his efforts to maintain toughness. Reed bites the corner of his lip, but he can't hold back his grin.

"I will do nothing." He said, before nudging his head in my direction. "She can handle herself. I was just warning you."

The guy glances at me. I can only picture what he's thinking. How could a 5'2 girl be worthy of a warning? They confirm my suspicions as he and his friends burst into laughter like cackling hyenas. I turn my lip in distaste and reach in my back for my trusted taser.

"Axel!"

Chelsea squeals running up to us. I drop my taser back in my bag as her arms wrap around the asshole. Reed seems as shocked as I am. He smirks at us over her shoulder. I clench my fists at my side.

"You already met Olivia!"

"I had no idea this was her." He reaches his hand out to me. I look at it as if it were a snake. "Pleasure meeting you, Olivia."

I squint my eyes at his sudden change in attitude. I wasn't buying it, but I didn't want to make a scene in front of Chelsea, so I shook his hand.

"And this is Reed."

Chelsea introduced him with less enthusiasm. He extends his hand again, but Reed tucks his hands in his pockets.

"What kind of name is Axel?"

I clap my hand over my mouth to hide my giggles. Chelsea's jaw drops.

"Reed!" she said. "What is wrong with you?"

"I'm just making conversation."

If looks could kill, Reed would have died. Even *Medusa* would cower at the stony stare.

"Well, go make it somewhere else."

This interaction between them is common, so I know he doesn't take it to heart. Chelsea grips Axel's hand.

"Let's go."

She offers me an apologetic look. I watch as she stomps off. Reed scoffs from behind me.

"He makes me look like a nice guy."

As much as I hate to admit it, he's right. Even from first appearances, Axel failed. What surprises me even more is that he's so beyond Chelsea's usual type. What's the appeal? I think back on my altercation with him before facing Reed.

"You didn't need to help me."

He grins and tucks his hands in his front pockets.

"Oh, I wasn't coming to help." He said. "I wanted front-row seats for the action."

Despite my best efforts, a subtle grin escaped.

"Well, next time I won't hesitate to bring out the taser."

"Promise?"

I don't know what I expected him to do. Maybe make an inappropriate comment about our kiss or tease me about how easy it was to get a rise out of me. Something childish, which is Reed's style.

"I'll see you later."

I was not expecting that.

He walks off, leaving me half expecting him to turn around and say he was joking. He didn't. His figure disappeared into the crowd, leaving me frozen.

Reed

I'm glad I did it. I'm glad I screwed with her head, even if it's going to bite me in the ass later. Knowing Olivia for a long time has given me insight into what sets her off. My acting out of character is going to have her head reeling. I feel giddy with anticipation, like waiting months for the next season of your favorite show.

St. James steps onto the stage, waving to the crowd as he's embraced with cheers. I roll my eyes, an unconscious habit every time I see him.

"How is everyone tonight?" He said into the microphone as if he was headlining *Madison Square Garden.*

He smiles as the crowd applauds him. What an asshole.

"I have a new song I've been working on." He said, looking into the crowd before his eyes landed on someone. "I wrote it for someone special."

He better be talking about his grandmother.

He leans closer to the microphone.

"This is for Olivia."

I resist the urge to vomit as he serenades her as if this were a cringe-worthy R*omcom.* I always hated them, but not as much as I hate him at this moment. My nose scrunches in disgust as Olivia seems to eat this up. She hated these kinds of things. She hated public declarations and always chastised these actions in every romance movie we'd watch. What's changed?

She watches him as if he'd hung the stars glimmering above us. What makes this so special? The movies already overused this. It's a stale cliché. I've witnessed him using this move on tons of girls before.

This is straight out of Wyatt St. James' playbook. I wanted to grab his guitar and hit him with it. *What a pretentious asshole.*

His song *finally* ends. The applause is rattling, and he soaks the attention up. Chelsea joins Olivia's side as they jump up and down. I roll my eyes before glancing away from the train wreck of a sight. I couldn't witness this any longer.

The stars glimmer towards the heavens, as midnight comes as a flawless black. Midnight is supposed to show an ending and a start. The end of yesterday, the start of today.

This time is the exception.

The party should have quieted down by now, but it seems it's getting livelier every hour that passes. The oversupply of alcohol eased everyone's inhibitions.

Except mine.

I couldn't find it in me to drink more than a cup. I wasn't feeling it tonight. The constant nagging thoughts in the back of my mind are a real buzzkill. The drunkards bothered me for the first time. I am used to joining them, not bearing witness to the travesty.

Why is this night endless?

I distance myself from the inebriated uproar and trail along the shoreline. The rhythmic movements of the water calm me down. My shoulders relax from the eased metaphorical weights. The sound of splashing fills my ears. I squint and see a girl running into the ocean a few feet away.

She's drunk.

I bolted towards the girl and pulled her out before she could go any further.

"Are you crazy?" I asked as I dragged her out. "Night swimming is dangerous."

I drag her further away from the ocean. The moonlight hits her face.

"Olivia," I said. "What is wrong with you?"

She clutches her head with a groan.

"Please stop yelling."

I'd barely raised my voice.

"Why are you alone out here?"

I glance around in case I've missed someone. She just shrugs, still clutching her head. A few tears escaped her eyes.

"I don't remember."

I run my fingers through my hair before sighing.

"Come on," I said. "Let's get you home and into bed."

I tuck my hands under her legs and torso before hoisting her into my arms. Her body is limp as if all the alcohol soaked into her muscles. She couldn't keep her eyes open. I mumble to myself as I haul her drunk ass all the way to the beach house. She only wakes up as I'm about to enter her bedroom.

"Put me down."

I roll my eyes at her ungrateful attitude. I should have made her walk by herself. I toss her onto the bed and pretend to dust my hands off, and I reach the doorway before she speaks again.

"This is all your fault, you know."

I look behind me, thinking she's talking to someone else, but we're the only two in the vicinity.

"Excuse me?"

"You're the reason I'm such a mess."

My shoulders tense as I step further into the room. I can't help but take offense.

"You got drunk all on your own," I said. "How is this *my* fault?"

She scoffs. Her hazy eyes lock with mine. Even when drunk, her eyes are like daggers.

"You broke me."

It's as if the alcohol was amplifying all her thoughts and emotions. If that's the case, she's pissed off with me. I clenched my jaw and looked at the ground.

"Look, I'm sorry, okay," I said and ran my fingers through my hair. "I made a mistake that night, and I will regret it forever."

I don't look at her, not wanting to see her reaction. I brace myself for the spiteful words.

They never come.

She'd passed out on her bed like a starfish. She probably didn't hear anything.

How infuriating.

I debate whether I should tuck her in, or smother her with a pillow, but my conscience overrules. I toss the sheets over her and place her trash bin near her bed. She'd most likely need it. I placed some *ibuprofen* on her bedside table and double-checked everything was in order before switching the lights off and closing the door. *She's going to regret this in the morning.*

17

Olivia

I have regretted nothing more in my entire life. The entire night after my strange encounter with Chelsea's new man, and the second strange encounter with Reed, was enough to send me spiraling. I needed an escape from my mind. I hadn't seen Wyatt the entire night, and that was enough to allow my impulsive thoughts to take over.

What a mistake that was.

I don't remember getting to bed. However, I'm thankful for the *ibuprofen* and the glass of water at my bedside.

It feels like *Travis Barker* is having a drum solo in my head.

I chug the pills and every drop of water before dragging myself into the bathroom and splashing cold water on my face, wishing I could wash away the poison in my body. I feel like I'm in an episode of *The Walking Dead* as I trundle downstairs. The smell of crispy bacon makes my stomach churn.

"Well, look who joined us."

Penelope's voice is like nails on a chalkboard. I clutch my head and take a seat at the counter.

"Are you hungover?" Marcus asked.

I can feel him approaching, but I don't move. The thought of his imminent lecture worsens my migraine.

"Now isn't the time, Marcus."

"Now is the perfect time." He said. "Look at me."

He nudges my arms, but I don't budge. His persistence is usually admirable but, at this moment, I find it insufferable.

"Can you stop?"

His nagging replaced my pain with annoyance as I lifted my head to glare at him.

"What were you thinking?"

It's like he thinks *he's* my father.

"I wanted to have fun for one night." I cross my arms over my chest. "Is that a crime?"

"You know you can't do that, Olivia."

His words irked me, and his accusatory tone ignited another level of bitterness. It pissed me off more than I ever could have imagined.

"Why? Because I'm your little sister?"

"Yes."

"You have no issue when Connor does it."

"That's because Connor wasn't-"

He halts in realization. My breath hitches in my throat. He didn't finish his sentence, but I know exactly what he was implying. The back of my eyes burns as I hold back my rage.

Will I ever escape the haunting past of last summer?

"Stop bringing it up."

The guilt is clear on his face, but I cannot muster any sympathy.

"I can't." He said. He's holding back tears of his own. "I can't pretend it never happened."

My bottom lip quivers, but I refuse to let him see me break. I clench my knuckles at my side until they become numb and shake my head before pushing myself off the stool. I needed distance.

"I can't either," I said as I strutted toward the large patio door. "Because everyone seems to get a kick out of bringing it up."

I open the door and slam it behind me. The fresh air does nothing to cool off my scorching face. I lean against the railing, close my eyes, and take deep breaths.

This is not what I had in mind first thing in the morning.

The sound of someone clearing their throat pulls me from my raging thoughts. I glance to my left and see Reed lying on the hammock with a beer firmly clutched in his hand. I'd chastise him for his early drinking, but he always had an answer to that. *It's late somewhere in the world.* As if Reed Adler ever needed an excuse to get into trouble.

"Are you going to lecture me, too?" I asked.

He'd been looking at me with an unreadable expression.

"No, you're not a little kid anymore."

"Tell that to Marcus."

He doesn't move from the hammock, instead; he swings it back and forth like you'd rock a baby to sleep.

"Marcus is only looking out for you."

"This seems like a lecture."

"Not at all." He said. "Just facts."

I don't speak. What is there to say? How am I supposed to find light when everyone keeps bringing up the darkness? How can I move on when the past keeps looming over me like a dark cloud ready to burst?

"There's nothing worse than watching the ones you love suffer." He said. "It affected Marcus more than you'd know."

I look at the cloudless sky, something I used to do often. The sun's rays reach out to me with the promise of lathering me in its warmth. All I had to do was grab it.

"How is anyone supposed to move on when he keeps bringing it up?"

"That wasn't something you can just forget, Olivia."

I'd heard enough. I've spoken about it enough. As *if I weren't the one with front-row seats to the drama.* I square my shoulders and take a deep, calming breath.

"I'm done with this conversation."

I turned my head before the trickle of tears ran down my cheeks. They may all be adamant about bringing up the past, but I'm determined to put it to the back of my mind and move forward.

Reed

There is one thing that always stayed the same during our summer in Cape May. The *Fourth of July Carnival.* We agreed in our younger years to never miss the tradition, and we've kept that pact strong.

This year is no exception.

The carnival is the epitome of nostalgia. From the overload of fried treats to the games, and to the main event fireworks show. Marcus and I never missed it.

Evening couldn't arrive fast enough. The moment the slanting rays of the setting sun cast long shadows on the beach, we rushed for the festivities. The carnivals have always been a sensory overload and rides were always lit up like *Times Square* during *New Year's*. All the aromas from the food stalls blended to create the ultimate mouth-drooling scent. My stomach growled in the desire for its annual feast. *Let the fun begin.*

"What are we doing first?" Marcus asked.

His arm is curled around Penelope's shoulders. Ever since their reconciliation, they have been attached to the hip. I wanted to feign disgust, but ever since my heart-to-heart with Penelope, she's become bearable.

"The rides first," Connor said, scrunching his nose. "I've learned my lesson."

We all laughed at the memory of last year. Connor had brought a girl along, eaten too much food, and threw up on her shoes after going on the ride. We'd warned him not to do it, but he can be stubborn. As we stood in a circle debating on what to do, Chelsea approached with her arms interlinked with her new beau.

"Sorry, we're late."

I glance at Olivia from the corner of my eye. She clenches her jaw so hard that it might crack. I had to bite the corner of my lip to hold back my smirk.

I've always loved it when she's heated.

It seems she's found someone she dislikes more than me. This is getting exciting. Olivia trails behind the group, glaring at the back of Axel's head. I strut to a similar pace beside her.

"Where's the boyfriend?"

"Spending the day with his family."

She avoids my gaze.

"Ouch," I said as I tucked my hands in my front pockets. "He didn't think to invite you with?"

"I wouldn't have gone, anyway."

"Not serious enough for meeting the family?"

"I guess not."

We don't speak for a while until I notice the Ferris Wheel in the distance. It towers over the entire carnival. I leaned closer to Olivia with a smirk.

"Doesn't that Ferris Wheel bring back so many memories?" I whisper into her ear so nobody else can eavesdrop. "The things we did up there could have gotten us into so much trouble, but it was worth it to hear your whimpers."

She shoves me with as much strength as she could muster, but it didn't matter. I chuckled at her perceivable anger. She wants me to think she's angered by my words, but she's angry because my words affected her in ways she didn't want. The goosebumps on her arms are a clarification to my theory.

I step away from her, pretending I never noticed a thing before jogging to keep up with Connor. However, I risk one more glance over my shoulder to find her eyes already set on me. She looks away. I bite my lip before looking forward.

I've got her where I want her.

18

Olivia

He's got me where he wants me, and that pisses me off. Giving Reed all the power is like giving *Voldemort* all the *Horcruxes*. It will just end in devastation.

We'd been at the carnival for about an hour before everyone split up. The couples wanted alone time, leaving the miserable singles alone… until Connor ditched us too.

"I'll see you later." He said before rushing to catch up to an unfamiliar girl.

"Who is that?"

"A girl he met at a tattoo parlor."

"Right, the tattoo he got because of you."

"He wanted to impress her."

He raises his hands in the air as if he's claiming innocence. I roll my eyes and walk away towards the games, but I can feel him shadowing me. I end up at the ring toss since it's the only one without a line.

"If you wanted me to win you a stuffed animal again, all you had to do was ask." He said into my ear.

I step aside and attempt to push those memories to the back of my mind. It's hard to believe it was over a year ago.

"I'd rather spend the rest of the night alone."

I abandon the game and strut away, but he follows me.

"Olive, you can't avoid me forever."

I whip around so fast that he barely halts in time before colliding into me.

"Stop calling me that."

He seems unaffected by my venomous outburst.

"You used to love when I called you that." He said, stepping closer to me and leaning his head down as if he were about to share a secret. "Especially when we were under the covers."

He reaches out to touch my cheek, but I slap his hand away.

"Don't. Touch. Me."

He cups his chin and squints his eyes as if in deep thought.

"That's funny. I don't remember you saying that when your tongue was down my throat in my bedroom."

My eyes widened. I'd waited for him to bring it up, but I never thought he would.

"That was a mistake."

I hoped to bruise his ego, but he's always been able to take a punch.

"Best mistake you've ever made."

My body tenses, as my blood feels as if someone lit a match internally.

"Leave me alone, Reed."

He bites the corner of his bottom lip.

"You're so sexy when you're angry."

Before he could garner another reaction out of me, I whipped around and speed walked as quickly as possible away from him. I sigh in relief as I don't hear his approaching footsteps or feel his looming presence. The moment I feel protected from his line of sight, I take a moment to compose myself. I place my hand over my rapid heart.

He got me again.

It took me longer than I wanted to regain my composure, but I did it in time to meet back up with the group. Penelope and Chelsea were gushing about how amazing their nights were, but something else distracted me as we lined up for the Ferris wheel. With Connor standing a few feet ahead with his arm slung over the tattoo girl's shoulder, the numbers have evened up. The thought sent a chill down my spine.

I'd have to go on the ride with Reed.

I glance ahead to find we'd be next. I had to get out of this.

"I'm not feeling well."

Everyone looks at me in shock.

"Don't tell me you're afraid." Connor said. "You love the Ferris wheel."

"It must have been something I ate."

It's the first thing that came to mind. I jump as Reed slings his arm over my shoulder, pulling me closer.

"Don't worry about it, Olive." He said. "I'll take care of you. Just like I did last year."

The rest might have found his comment harmless, but I picked up on his sly innuendo. I didn't want to make a scene. It would raise suspicion. Instead, I mustered a grin and followed them up the stairs to get on the ride. I slide into the seat, but I get squished as Reed slithers as close as possible to me.

"Give me some space."

I attempt to nudge him with my elbow, which prompts him to move closer.

"I just want to make sure you feel safe."

"We both know that's not why I tried to get out of this."

"Don't worry, I know why," He said. "You're trying to fight the urge to have a repeat of last time."

I stiffen.

"I have no idea what you're talking about."

"The last time we were on this very Ferris wheel." He said and placed a hand on my thigh.

I choke on the air before pushing his hand away. His words ignite unwanted memories. The memories I've tried so hard to push away. It's as if I were reliving the exact moment. The feel of his warm hand on my bare thigh and the goosebumps ignited just by a simple touch. I think back on the sneaky kisses and the sinful touches, the desperation for any form of relief before the ride descended.

Every feeling I'd tried so hard to hold down seemed to have broken free. My want and desire for him had become magnified as the déjà vu setting made it more real.

It's as if I was experiencing one of the best moments of my life all over again.

The instant his hand returned to my thigh; my cord of resistance snapped. My desires sprung to life, and I attached my lips to his. Surprise took him before putting his hand behind my head. He deepens the kiss and draws me closer.

His hands slide up my thigh and under my dress. I groan not only in pleasure, but anticipating what is to come. I almost giggle at the irony. His fingers glide all over the right places. I groan in his mouth before he pulls away. Desire glazed in his eyes, the very look he had on this exact day, in this exact spot, one year ago.

His fingers slid into my underwear before I could react. I gasp as he brushes against all the right spots. My stomach clenches in desire as I release a guttural moan. He leans to whisper in my ear.

"Try to be quiet." He said. "We wouldn't want to let on how good I've always been able to make you feel."

I bite my lip as his movements become more deliberate. I clutch the handles of the seat as I arch my head back. Each touch is like an electric shock.

I spread my legs further, which encourages his movements. All the tension I've been holding in gets diminished with each brush of his fingers. I can feel my imminent release bubbling up in my stomach as every muscle in my body tightens. My eyes closed so tight I saw stars. I get closer and closer every second.

Until the feeling fades away.

My eyes snap open. I look at Reed with mortified eyes and bated breath. Why did he stop? I only realize once we reach the bottom. My cheeks are flushed, and I can only imagine what my physical appearance must look like. I stand on shaky legs as we exit the ride and join the others.

265

"Olivia, your cheeks are so red," Penelope said, moving closer and placing her hand on my forehead like a concerned mother. "You're burning up."

I risk a glance at Reed. He tucked his hands in his front pockets as he looked down at his shoes. He's trying his best not to laugh.

"I think I just need to rest."

"Let's get you home."

I glance over my shoulder as the rest of the group follows. My eyes lock with Reed's. He drops his left eye in a wink before joining Marcus and Connor's conversation.

Did I just allow that to happen again?

Reed

I could barely look Marcus in the eye the entire time we were training at the rink. He kept bringing up how much fun he had at the carnival last night. How he enjoyed quality time with Penelope.

"What did you get up to?" He asked. "Anything exciting happen?"

Other than having my fingers between your sister's legs? Nothing much.

"Nothing exciting."

I avoid his eyes and focus on twirling the stick in my hand. It's as if I feared he could sense my immoral thoughts by looking into my eyes. I know I'm being ridiculous, but the guilt is eating me alive.

That was the only downfall of being with Olivia.

"Well, Olivia is going on a date with Wyatt today."

My head shoots up.

"How do you know?"

"Penelope told me." He made a face. "He texted her this morning and Penelope insisted on helping her get ready."

I nearly snapped my hockey stick in half from my taut grip. The tip of my ears burned. I couldn't believe she'd agree to a date with him. Was he on her mind while she was spreading her legs for me on the Ferris wheel?

I doubt it.

I take a deep breath through my nose.

"Who cares?" I said, feigning disinterest. "Enough chatting. It's time for me to kick your ass."

He grins at my words, a silent acceptance of my challenge.

"Just don't cry again if I hit you with my stick."

I roll my eyes at his jab.

"We were five." I said. "Are you ever going to let that go?"

He always slides that embarrassing event into every hockey conversation. His dad took us to the rink after we'd expressed an interest in playing hockey. It was the first time we'd ever been on the ice. I was standing behind Marcus and he swung the stick too far back and hit me on the lip. I screamed the moment I saw blood. He felt so guilty then, but now it's become an outdated joke.

"I'll never let you forget it."

He grins before stealing the puck from me and skating off. I chase after him as my competitiveness takes over.

This is what I need to forget about everything, even if it's only for a little while.

I'd gotten a text from Brynlee inviting me to another beach party her friend was hosting. The idea is lacking in originality, but it beats sitting at home doing nothing. Connor and Chelsea accepted the offer without hesitation, but it took a while longer to convince Penelope and Marcus. They insisted they wanted to stay at home and binge watch movies like an old married couple, but my skills of persuasion reeled them in.

However, the moment we arrived, they'd all ditched me, leaving me sitting by the bonfire with a bunch of strangers. The Driftwood log seats were uncomfortable. I kept fidgeting and directing my angered gaze on the fire as if it were the reason for my uneasiness.

A red cup blocks the fire, and I reach out for it. I could tell who it was just by her luminous yellow nails. Brynlee slouches next to me.

"You look like you need it."

"I do." I take a sip. "Thanks."

We don't speak as we analyze our surroundings, judging the group of drunk guys a few feet away. They were so out of it they couldn't fathom they were shouting over each other despite their huddled proximity. We could hear every word.

"She's going to give in soon." The guy with the buzz cut and shitty tattoos speaks. "It hasn't been very hard."

They all laugh as if he were a master comedian instead of an arrogant jackass. I don't make a sound as I wait for him to say more.

"Once I'm done with Chelsea, I'm going to give Monica a text."

My head snaps up at the sound of the familiar name. I scope the guy's appearance. My eyes widen as he turns his head to the side, granting me a view of his face.

It's Chelsea's guy. Axel.

My shoulders stiffened as he and his group of buddies cackled at his words. One of them catches my stare and his laughter halts.

"What are you looking at?" He asked, making all his friend's heads turn.

"Hey, you're Chelsea's buddy." Axel said, as if he wasn't just making crude remarks about her.

I stand up, despite Brynlee trying to push me back. I tuck my hands at my side.

"We're not friends," I said. "But it still pisses me off how you just spoke about her."

His relaxed composure tensed, as if my words had triggered him.

"What's that got to do with you?"

His indifferent attitude vexes me. I step closer until we're face to face. I tower over him.

"You don't want to piss me off right now."

I must give him credit. He doesn't flinch.

"Look, go be a hero somewhere else," He said. "Whoever I bring into my bed is of no concern to you."

I clench my fingers into a fist so hard they go numb.

"It is when you're talking about someone I know."

"Look, if she didn't want me to fuck her, then she wouldn't dress like such a slut around me."

Everything around me turned red. My emotions heightened. The moment it's triggered, it's tough to hold it back. My cursed impulsiveness kicks in. I don't think about the repercussions. I don't think about how I'm outnumbered. All I think about is driving my fist into his jaw. *That's what I do.*

19

Olivia

The sunset reflects against the infinite sea, its beauty running to the ends of the Earth. Despite the surrounding commotion, it feels as if it's only Wyatt and me on this beach. I'd dreaded meeting up with him after my traitorous interactions with Reed, but despite it all, Wyatt can still make my stomach flutter. We stroll along the shore with interlocked fingers, avoiding the buzzing party a few feet away. I become distracted by the bewitching waves.

"I had a great day with you." Wyatt said. "It's been a while since I've had so much fun."

I glance at him with a giddy smile.

"I feel the same."

I ignore the churning of my stomach and hold his hand tighter. My stomach sinks even further when he pulls away from my hold.

"I need to ask you something."

I don't speak. *I can't.* The severity of his tone makes me anxious. I can only muster a nod. He inhales deeply.

"What would you say if I told you I was hanging out with someone else?"

My stomach drops like an avalanche. The ambivalence of emotions I feel makes me dizzy.

Did he just imply what I think he did? Or am I overthinking it?

My brain pounds against my skull as if it has its own heartbeat. I didn't know what to say. I've never been one for casual relationships, although I've only ever been in one. Would it benefit me to try something new? Maybe I'd realize casual is better for me. Less drama and fewer chances of getting hurt.

I've done serious, and it ended in heartbreak.

Am I willing to go through that again?

A commotion a few feet away diverted my attention before I could speak. The overcapacity of people in the huddle prevented me from seeing what they were bolting towards. However, the moment I saw Connor and Marcus bolting towards it, I knew only one person could cause the chaos. I push through the crowd until I get front-row seats to the unexpected action. Axel was the last person I imagined Reed fighting. They've spoken once.

Once is enough for Reed, I guess.

Axel and his friends outnumbered Reed until Marcus and Connor came to his rescue. *Again.* Axel's buddies backed off the moment they evened the playing field, but Reed and Axel weren't quite done. They'd both fallen on the sand as they delivered punch after punch. Marcus rushed to pull Reed away, but he'd landed one last punch to Axel's nose. I winced at the *crack*.

"Axel!" Chelsea said, rushing to him.

I didn't even notice her presence. She placed her hand on his shoulder as he clutched his nose. I looked away the moment I saw blood escaping.

"What is your problem, Reed?"

He's crouched over, clutching his jaw.

"It's just a broken nose. It will heal."

Even I shiver at her icy gaze. I don't think I've ever seen Chelsea so enraged.

"Are you kidding me?" She asked. "How about I break your nose so you can see how it feels?"

Even with the blood dripping down his left cheek, he still finds the energy to piss her off.

"Take your best shot."

She groans before dragging Axel away. The crowd disperses once they realize the drama is over.

"What was that about?" Marcus asked.

Reed shrugs and wipes the blood away. His eyes glance to his left before turning to Marcus.

"I didn't like the way he was looking at me."

So, he ruined my best friend's chances of happiness for something so tedious? Sure, Axel didn't give off the best first impression, but it's no reason to hit him.

"You are seriously an asshole, Adler." He glances at me with wide eyes, as if he did not know I was standing there. "You may have ruined Chelsea's relationship before it even started."

He opens his mouth to say something but immediately closes it and shrugs as if he didn't give a damn.

It's because he doesn't.

I tear my gaze away, unable to be in the same vicinity as him any longer. He always does this. He reels me in and then does something selfish, reminding me of why we ended. I turn and stomp off, ignoring everyone's calls for me to come back. I needed to get away from civilization, even if I didn't know where I was going. But someone was making it near impossible.

"Olivia!"

I turn as the girl I've seen Reed hanging out with bolts in my direction. It doesn't take her long to catch up with me.

"Hi," she said. "I'm Brynlee."

I put a name to the face.

"Olivia." I said, even though she clearly knows it.

"Look, I'm going to cut to the chase." She said, tucking a wavy strand of hair behind her ear. "Reed didn't fight that guy for no reason."

I raise my brow.

"That guy was saying some really crude stuff about your friend." She said. "He took it too far and Reed got pretty upset."

I scan her face. Either she's telling the truth, or she has the greatest poker face in history.

"Why wouldn't he say that?"

She scoffs.

"You know him better than I do." She said. "Even I know Reed would never admit to doing something good."

She has a point. Reed would rather gauge his own eyes out before showing that side of him. The side I'd never have believed he had if I'd never witnessed it firsthand.

"Why are you telling me this?"

She looks at me as if I've asked the dumbest question ever.

"He's in love with you."

Her unexpected words are like a knockout punch.

"I have no idea what you're talking about."

She snorts.

"He told me about last summer."

My eyes inflate like a hot-air balloon. I try to bluff, but it's obvious my reaction gives it away.

"Don't worry." She raises her hands. "Your secret is safe with me."

I wanted to believe her. Why would Reed confess to a random stranger?

"Even the one where you're still in love with him, too."

Correction, *that* was the knockout punch. Who says something like that to someone they've just met?

"Look, I know I don't know you." She said, as if she's a mind reader. "I barely know Reed, but I know he messed up."

I nod in agreement.

"We're all going to get hurt. It's inevitable. Those who care will fix it, those who don't will break us." She said. "Reed is putting in an effort to make up for what he did. That's got to count for something."

She leaves me to process her words to the point it feels as if my brain has malfunctioned. The staggering thoughts gave me a migraine until they bundled up into one thought.

Can I forgive last summer's betrayal?

Reed

I look like shit, but at least I look better than that douchebag, Axel. I look at myself in the mirror, grinning in satisfaction despite the pain from my split lip. The only regret I have is letting him have a lucky shot. I run my hands under the cold water before splashing some on my face. I'm still too heated. To distract my raging thoughts, I dig in the first aid kit for something to soothe my aching lip. I find alcohol wipes, not hesitating to clean the cut. I wince a few times.

"Let me help with that."

Penelope's reflection appears in the mirror. My shoulders tense as I lean against the counter waiting for the impending lecture, but it never comes. Neither of us speaks as she dabs at my cut, being as gentle as if I were a newborn. She must have felt my stare, as glances at me from under her lashes with a half-smile.

"If you'd have told me a week ago, I would help to treat your wounds after a fight. I'd have laughed in your face."

"So, why are you helping me?"

I wasn't asking to be malicious. It flabbergasted me on why she'd be the one to help me.

"Pretend our conversation never happened, but it did." She said. "I guess I've seen the Reed Adler that Marcus always speaks of."

I raise my brow in disbelief.

"Don't act so surprised." She said. "Marcus always used to stick up for you. He once told me I'd have to wait and see for myself, and it seems I have."

Her words warm my heart. I'd braced myself for a scolding, especially from Penelope. *It's not a good time to be optimistic.* I remind myself, knowing that Olivia and Chelsea are thinking of all the ways they could kill me right now.

"He's said the same thing about you," I said as she packed everything back into the kit. "I thought he was just being a wonderful boyfriend, but when you're not yelling down my throat, you are kind of cool."

She chuckles at my words, something she never used to do. *Perhaps we've found common ground.*

"So, want to explain why you went into *ultimate fighter* mode?"

She places her hands on her hips. This was the first time she'd questioned my actions instead of assuming my guilt.

"That Axel guy is an asshole."

"You're an asshole, but I've always resisted the urge to punch you."

I sighed and tilted my head back with closed eyes.

"He was saying some crap about Chelsea," I said. "He boasted to his friends about his plan to sleep with her and then end things."

She raises her brow.

"You've done that countless times."

"I don't brag about it to my friends," I said. "And I don't feel good about doing it either."

"So, why keep doing it, then?"

I mull over her words. I know why, but am I ready to say it out loud? To Penelope, of all people? I can't explain why I did it without revealing what happened with Olivia last summer. If I tell Penelope, she will tell Marcus. Keeping it a secret would require lying to Marcus. That's not how their relationship works. I refuse to put her in that position.

"It's just easier that way," I said. "That way you don't get attached."

She bites her bottom lip.

"Sounds lonely to me." She said. "Despite everything, I couldn't picture a day without Marcus."

I push myself from the counter and fold my arms across my chest.

"That's because Marcus is a great guy."

I brushed past her in a rush to leave this conversation, but her words stop me in the doorway.

"So are you. You just don't want to believe it." She said. "The only one holding you back is you."

I drop my head and amble to my room in dire need of solitude. I fall onto my bed, ignoring the aches in my muscles, and close my eyes as Penelope's words echo in my mind. Deep down, I know she's right, but I've always gravitated to self-sabotage. No matter how much I fight it, I can never escape my demons.

20

Olivia

The walk was insightful. The surrounding darkness blocked out all distractions, leaving me with only my thoughts. I didn't realize how long I'd been walking until I'd gazed up at the sky. The stars faded from exhaustion after the long night.

My thoughts evolved around Wyatt and his unforeseen question. *He wanted to see other people.* Was I not good enough for him? It's the only reason I can think of. If he liked me, he wouldn't be looking for other connections elsewhere. I'm not his girlfriend. It's sensible for him to consider his options since we've only recently met. Yet, my nagging insecurities kept telling me it was because I was not good enough.

I expected the house to be silent. Everyone is likely asleep, preparing for the upcoming day. I didn't expect the living room to be illuminated by the kitchen light, or to hear rustling.

Marcus was digging in the back of the refrigerator. I cleared my throat, alerting him to my presence. His head shot up, hitting the shelf above him. I bite my lip as he clutches the back of his head. His eyes narrow in on me as I choke back a laugh.

"I've been waiting for you." He said.

"I just needed to clear my head."

"Anything I need to worry about?"

I couldn't help but smile. Marcus is always an overbearing older brother, even in the worst of times.

"No," I said. "But I know you will, anyway."

He chuckles before walking around the counter. He ruffles my hair and I slap his hand away. *I always hated it when he did that.*

"Get some rest." He said, sounding like mom. "I'll see you in the morning."

I never realized how exhausted I was until the trek upstairs drained me. My eyelids were being anchored by sleep. They burned as my bedroom light seemed as bright as the sun, and squinted as I hurried to my dresser, eager to get ready for bed. I slipped my shirt off to replace it with a new one, but a presence on my bed caught me unawares. I reach for the shirt on the ground and place it in front of my body.

Reed is resting on my bed, with his hands behind his head. He's grinning from ear to ear as if he'd gotten a personal striptease. I waited for him to say something, but my patience wore thin.

"What are you doing here?" I asked as quietly as possible. "Why didn't you tell me you were here the moment I walked in?"

He shrugs but keeps his casual pose.

"It seems less fun that way."

I rolled my eyes and put my shirt back on, ignoring his penetrating gaze. I fold my arms across my chest and wait for him to give me a logical reason for being in my room.

"I've forgotten how comfortable this bed is."

He sank further into the mattress. I grab a pillow at the end of my bed and chuck it as hard as I can to him, but his reflexes are too fast as he catches it.

"That was rude."

Now he's just trying to antagonize me.

"Why are you here?"

"I'm staying here for the summer."

Now I know he's trying to piss me off.

"You know that's not what I meant," I said. "I meant my bedroom."

"Oh." He pretends to be dumbfounded. "Was maybe hoping for some nostalgia."

"Well, leave."

"We've hardly spent any time together." He said with a pout, as if it would make me swoon.

"There's a reason for that."

I wait for him to take the hint and leave, but he remains motionless on my bed. With burning frustration, I grab my stuff to get changed in the bathroom. He places his hand over mine on the door handle. I freeze up as I feel his frame pressing up against my back.

How did he get here so fast?

I close my eyes as the hairs on the back of my neck rise. He was close enough for me to feel his breath on my face. I could even hear it.

"I've been waiting for you to scold me." He whispered in my ear. "You were taking too long."

My mouth feels dry, and my throat feels closed off.

"Scold you about what?"

"The fight."

He doesn't move away. In fact, it felt like he'd gotten even closer, caging me between himself and the door.

"Whatever you do is none of my business."

I shiver as his lips brush against my earlobe.

"That's a shame." He said. "I've always loved it when you put me in my place."

I felt comatose as his hand slid up my arm before tucking strands of hair away from my neck. I close my eyes as he leans closer, but he doesn't touch me further.

"Spending a summer with you was a bad idea." He said in my ear. "Ever since our kiss, I can't resist myself."

My stomach clenched as an unfamiliar feeling washed over me.

This is like last summer.

No matter how much I tried to resist him, he always cast me under his spell with just a simple touch. History is repeating itself. I turned around in his arms, glancing up at him with pleading eyes. I'm pleading for him to resist the temptation because I don't think I can.

"Do you remember all the late nights we used to spend here?" He breathes against my neck. "When we'd wait until everyone was asleep."

My breath quivers. He trails his fingers from my shoulders, over the top of my breasts, before sliding down my stomach, gripping my hips, and pulling me closer to him. He leans down until our lips brush.

"I miss those nights so much."

His lips caressed mine before he kissed me with purpose. It's as if he'd sucked the air out of me, along with my thoughts. His hand's warmth seeped through my shirt. Familiarity didn't diminish the excitement.

I cupped the back of his neck to draw him in closer as if his kisses were my life support. I disregard the consequences when I'm with him. He's like the devil on my shoulder, convincing me to choose the immoral side. I groan as his lips trail kisses down my neck.

Immorality has never felt so right.

I bit his bottom lip, consumed by the taste of him. Until the knock on my door.

"Olive, are you okay?" Connor's voice echoes from under the door.

I recoil from Reed and shove him toward the bathroom door.

"Hide," I whispered before speed-walking to talk to Connor.

His concerned expression was obvious, even with the dim lighting.

"You weren't home when I got back." He said. "I saw your light was still on and wanted to see if you're okay."

It's rare that Connor was the concerned brother. He cares, but he's accustomed to being the youngest.

"I'm good, just needed to clear my head. Getting ready for bed now."

He scopes my face for any hint of dishonesty before nodding. Leaning down, he kisses the top of my head. I have a year on him, and he still towers over me.

"I'll see you in the morning."

I don't move until he's in his room with the door shut behind him. The moment I turn around, Reed attaches his lips to mine again. *I can't let this happen again.* I pull away by placing my hands on his chest.

"Stop," I said. "This shouldn't have happened."

He furrows his brows as if I'd offended him.

"Please tell me you're kidding."

"I'm not, Reed." I sigh. "We cannot have a repeat of last summer."

"No one ever suggested a repeat."

"It's pretty obvious that's what's happening."

He runs his fingers through his hair. He always does that when he's upset.

"Please tell me what to say."

"I don't want you to say anything," I said. "You need to leave."

His jaw clenches as if he wants to say more, but he's holding back. He shakes his head before brushing past me. He slams his bedroom door with so much anger that I'm sure he woke up the entire neighborhood.

The choice may not have been right, but it's for the best.

Reed

I'm unsure why I went into her room. I waited for hours for her to come home and give me an earful, but her lack of arrival worried me. Afraid something had happened to her. Entering her room was a terrible choice. As I waited, all the memories rose to the surface like high tide.

All the late nights sneaking into her bedroom, taking up every second I had to hold her in my arms until it was time for me to return to my room. Or the way she would force me to watch a show she'd become obsessed with, or how she'd drone on about a new book she'd read. *It was all worth it because I got to be with her.* I had it all and then I ruined it. Because I'm a self-destructive asshole.

Trying is crucial, even if my actions cannot be forgiven. I can't undo what happened last summer, but I can make amends. It's better than nothing. It's one of the few ways I can show I still care. Because as much as I pretend, I'm still in love with her.

I never stopped loving her. I even have a tattoo as a constant reminder. *July 14th.* My birthday. Also, the day I first told Olivia I loved her. It feels like a lifetime ago. In just 24 hours, that day will come again. Except, I don't have my girl this time.

"You've been daydreaming a lot."

Marcus' voice shatters my veil of thoughts. I ignore his comment and take in his appearance. I thought I'd woken up early, but he was already dressed for the day.

"Going somewhere?"

He shrugs.

"Just doing some errands."

I raise my brow with a smirk.

"Do these involve getting everything set up for a certain tradition?"

Every year, on the day before my birthday, Marcus would host a gigantic party at the beach house. He'd invite everyone he knew, and through word of mouth, the party would reach maximum capacity.

He may have gotten more boring since meeting Penelope, but he knows how to throw a party.

"I have no idea what you're talking about."

He's as transparent as the air.

"You've always been a terrible liar."

He rolls his eyes.

"I'll see you later."

His fading footsteps are replaced with another. I freeze as Olivia turns the corner. She mimics my action the moment she realizes I'm in the room. She clears her throat.

"Morning."

"Morning."

She leans against the counter furthest from me. Her eyes dart everywhere but in my direction. I hold back my smug grin.

"What are your plans for your birthday?"

Is this her lame attempt at conversation? If so, it's best to indulge her.

"Same as every year. I'm spending it with the special people in my life." I said. "So, you better be there."

Her eyes widened at my words. She opens and closes her mouth like a goldfish before pretending to reach for a glass above her. I see an opportunity to sneak up on her and I take it, cornering her between myself and the counter, like last night.

I'm loving this position.

"What are you doing?"

"I need a glass, too."

I grab one for her and myself. She turns around and I place the glass in her hand. I wink before creating as much distance as possible. I fill my cup to the brim with water and raise it to my lips before spilling it down my shirt.

"That's cold."

My acting skills could win me an *Oscar*. I reach for the hem of my shirt and slowly raise it above my head. I sneak a quick glance at her to see she's watching my every move. She wasn't being subtle. I cleared my throat once I noticed her eyes lingering on my new tattoo. She looks away with reddened cheeks.

"I have to go." She said, before bolting out of the kitchen and back upstairs.

I hide my smirk behind my glass before taking a sip of the leftover water.

"What's got you smiling so early in the morning?" Connor asked.

He fluffs his hair and slumps on a chair by the counter. He's never been a morning person.

"Nothing at all."

21

Olivia

Snap out of it, Olivia. The plan was to stay away from him, not ogle him. It had been a while since I'd been so close to his shirtless torso. I'd gotten distracted by the newest additions to his skin.

Especially one tattoo in particular.

I divided my brain between thinking it was only his birthday and hoping for something related to that day.

Talk about a dream.

The relentless buzzing of my phone saves me from my consuming thoughts. Only for a moment. Wyatt's name and face illuminate my screen. I'd forgotten about our devastating conversation. The one where I'd bored him to where he needed other options. The thought should have made me upset, but it enraged me.

Why bother with a guy who isn't interested in exclusivity? I've never been one of those girls that explored her options. When I like someone, I like only them. When did that part of me change?

I did not direct my anger at Wyatt. I directed it at me. I'm doing the exact thing. I keep telling Wyatt how much I like him before locking lips with my ex-boyfriend. How can I judge him for exploring his options? I place my head in my hands and groan into them.

"What's going on?" Chelsea asked.

I jumped at her voice. She's hovering in my doorway clad in the bikini she deems *boy-catching worthy.*

"Where are you going?" I asked, hoping to steer the conversation away from my despair.

She knows me better than that. She folds her arms across her chest and juts out her hip. Just from those actions alone, I could sense her telepathic disbelief.

"Wyatt suggested we see other people."

I ripped the *Band-Aid* off, bracing myself for the scarring.

"What?" Her scream would make a banshee envious. "I'm going to punch him in his pointy nose."

I wanted to laugh and cry, but I repressed any emotions. I didn't want to dwell on the disappointment.

"At least he's honest," I said. "Let's forget about it. We need to get ready for tonight."

She curls her top lip.

"I don't think I'm going to Reed's party." She said. "I refuse to celebrate his birth."

I snort. She's always been overdramatic. She's never been one to miss a party, and she won't stop that streak soon.

FOMO.

"Whatever you say."

I grin, not believing her.

"I'm meeting up with Axel soon."

My smile drops. Brynlee's warnings against Axel flicker into my mind. Do I tell Chelsea? Or will that cause more unnecessary drama? I intended to tell her, but a knock on the door interrupted me.

"I'll get it."

Chelsea grinned before bolting as quickly as she could in her high heels. I will never understand how she doesn't break an ankle.

"Oh, it's you."

"Is Olivia here?"

I save myself from falling off the stool at the familiar voice. *Wyatt.* I risk a peek around the corner, only to be busted. Wyatt was looking over Chelsea's shoulder at me. I wave before moving from my terrible hiding spot.

"I'll leave you to talk."

Chelsea closes the door behind her. We stood in the hallway. It's as silent as a funeral procession. We want to say something, but we're afraid of hurting someone's feelings.

"I'm sorry."

"Why are you apologizing?"

"For the things I said."

"You don't need to apologize. You were being honest."

I glance down at the floor, knowing my eyes won't back up my words. I felt conflicted, wanting to embrace him or punch him.

"I know, but my honesty hurt you." He said. "It was never my intention."

I won't beg him to be with me. My plan was to be spontaneous. This is the summer of new experiences.

"I forgive you and I'm over it."

"Really?"

"Really."

His shoulders slump as if he were bearing a hefty weight of guilt. He had a genuine look at not wanting to hurt me.

"I'm hoping I can make it up to you?" He asked. "We could go out for dinner?"

I bit my lip.

"I have plans," I said. "Reed's birthday party. I'd invite you, but I know how you feel about each other."

He nods.

"I'd rather not." He said. "Raincheck?"

I nod my head, dreading that I couldn't be with him tonight. Yet, I made promises, and I never broke them. I close my eyes as he leans down to place a chaste kiss on my cheek.

I sigh as he walks out the door, not in sadness, but in despair. I had no inclination to chase after him.

It felt too much like a rave. The smell of beer and pungent marijuana invaded my nostrils. It was so overpowering, as if someone had shut all the windows and doors to keep the smell trapped inside.

I glanced down at the cherry red rug on the floor, now splattered in an abundance of alcohol and cigarette ash. It was my mom's favorite rug.

I was uncertain if it was the loud music or the second-hand high, but I had to escape. I bolted when someone opened the sliding door. I breathed in the air as if it were in short supply.

"Couldn't handle it either?"

I took in Brynlee's relaxed posture on our porch swing. She moved over and patted the spot beside her, gesturing for me to join her.

"Tonight is not my night."

I slide in next to her. We sit in silence and watch the stars as if it were the most interesting reality show ever. The gentle rocking of the swing is soothing, like a mother rocking their newborn. A change in surroundings is what I needed.

"It's nice that despite everything, you're still here to celebrate Reed's birthday." She said.

I look at her out of my peripherals.

"What do you mean?"

"He told me you had quite the nasty breakup." She leaned back in her seat. "He didn't go into detail, and I didn't press him for it."

I roll my eyes.

"Let me guess, he played the victim."

She turns to me with widened eyes.

"He only blames himself."

It's now my turn to look at her as if she'd grown an extra head.

"You're kidding."

"You know I'm not."

I glance at her, uncertain of her tone.

"What are you trying to say?"

"If he's as awful as you claim, you wouldn't have fallen for him."

I take in her words of wisdom. The voice in my head screamed against the truthful thoughts. I always try to downplay Reed's natural goodness. The bitter part of me can't seem to shake off his betrayal. It's as if that one mistake trumped all the good he's done.

It was a colossal mistake, though. The rational side of me speaks. *Yet, some mistakes are worth forgiving.*

"He hurt me."

I spoke into the wind, forgetting Brynlee was still beside me.

"Love hurts." She said. "I'm sure what he did was fucked up, but it's obvious you both care."

Is it?

I remember how different this day was a year ago. What a contrast. Our epic love ended in a tragedy that would put *Romeo and Juliet* to shame. Should I stop focusing on the past and think of the possibilities? *Perhaps I should let all inhibitions go, even if it's only for tonight.*

"You're right."

I doubt she even had time to register my words before rushing off. I promised myself a summer free from overthinking, and I'm going to stick to it. No matter the consequences.

Reed

I wanted to enjoy myself. This is, hands down, the best birthday party Marcus has hosted, but I couldn't help thinking about how many things could go wrong. Someone has damaged the carpets and burned cigarette holes in the curtains. They spilled multiple drinks in the living room alone.

Mrs. Huxley is going to kill us.

I don't know how many trips I've taken to the keg for a refill, but I hardly feel buzzed. The off-season is the only time I can get away with drinking an abundance of alcohol and passing out without the stress of practice the next day. It's all ruined by this off-brand beer. It seemed to have the opposite effect on Connor as he limped his way to join me in my corner crevice. His glossy eyes float around the room as if he were seeing everything for the first time.

"You're a mess."

I chuckle as he slouches against the wall.

"And you're boring."

He attempts to point an accusatory finger in my direction, but he misses the mark. I moved his hand, so it's pointed at me.

"I think we need to get you some water."

He shakes his head for longer than necessary as his gaze seems far away. I look over my shoulder, wondering what could have piqued his interest, but I only see Marcus, Penelope, and a few of her friends. She's the first to notice us, and even from a distance, I know she can sense Connor's intoxicated posture.

"That girl is checking me out."

"That would be Penelope."

"Oh," he said in disappointment. "Why is she looking at me like that, then?"

"You mean in utter shame?"

He shakes his head as if his brain is stuck. He blinks a few times before licking his chapped lips.

"I need fresh air."

I watch as he walks away in the opposite direction from the outside, not saying a word as he waltzes into the kitchen.

He'll figure it out.

The compact room was becoming unbearable. The staircase was closer than the outside, so I took the easy alternative. I needed an escape for a moment, some privacy to pack some things out of my mind. I abandoned my drink and ascended the staircase, taking my time strutting down the hallway to my bedroom, knowing that there would be no one upstairs to disturb me.

I was wrong.

I jumped at the icy hand on my arm before someone yanked me into a bedroom. I regained my balance after a few stumbles. My eyes popped out of its sockets, as if I were in an

313

episode of *Tom and Jerry*. Olivia was the one that pulled me. Into her room. I didn't know what to expect. Perhaps I pissed her off again.

Like breathing.

I don't say a word. She was the one that dragged me in here, so I'm owed an explanation.

"Don't speak." She said.

I debate on running out of the room the moment she reaches behind her back and unzips her dress before letting it drop to the floor. I glance behind me as if I'd entered an alternate universe, or I was an apparition having an *out-of-body* experience.

"Are you talking to me?"

Despite the shock, I couldn't help but let my eyes trail down her barely covered body. It's been a long time since she graced me with this sight, and I would not let the opportunity slip. My eyes trail down her neck, lingering on her breasts before scaling down the curvature of her hips, until I reach her thighs. No inch of skin goes unnoticed by me.

"Are you that much of an idiot, Reed?"

She folds her arms across her chest. I twitch at the sight of her prominent cleavage. I tear myself from the lust and focus on her eyes. Is she drunk? High? Had she hit her head and gotten amnesia, causing her to forget the past year? All the possibilities were endless.

"What's going on, Olivia?"

Despite the prominent sexual atmosphere, my organs twist at her uncharacteristic behavior.

"I just want to forget."

"Forget what?"

"All the pain of the past year." She said. "I want to relive that night."

I know she's talking about last year. The day that changed our entire relationship. *One of our last happy moments.*

"Olivia, you're worrying me."

I want nothing more than to relive that night, but not like this.

"You can't tell me today hasn't stirred up those feelings."

Was she reading my mind?

"Of course, they have."

"Good," she said. "Then come closer."

Like an invisible string pulling me, I stepped forward until I was one step away from taking her in my arms. I scope her eyes for any sign of hesitancy or regret, but her eyes twinkle with so much passion and lust. I could only imagine my eyes burning like the sun. She places her hands on my chest before trailing her fingers down to my belt. I clench my stomach in anticipation. But she doesn't move.

"Lock the door."

I shiver as she steps back, my body already craving her warmth again. I locked the door before rushing back to have her in my arms again, afraid that she'd changed her mind during our brief departing. She must have thought the same as she latched onto me. Our lips found each other like magnets. It was as if the past year had never happened, our kisses filled with as much passion as ever before. The flame never died out.

Her hand clutching the back of my head was like fuel to the fire. My fingers ghosted along her sides until they rested on her hips. She gasped as I gripped her bare skin. There was no hesitancy, no miscommunications. We both knew each other's bodies as if they were our own. I remember every freckle on her body, every sensitive spot, every insecurity she'd had.

So much about her has changed, but it all feels the same. My adoration for her never dwindled. In fact, our long-term separation magnified my infatuation for her. I'd been so enamored by thoughts of herthat that I never realized she'd removed my shirt until her nails scratched along my abdomen.

"I missed this." She said. "I missed you."

My knees buckled at her words.

"You have no idea how much I missed you." I pull away to look into her eyes so she can see the severity of my words. "I tried everything I

317

could to forget you, but you're difficult to forget."

22

Olivia

My impulsive decision holds multiple consequences. However, the intensity swimming in his eyes drowns all my concerns. I would deal with the aftermath.

Our rekindling is like muscle memory. I trail my fingers along his abdomen as I take in every detail of him, especially the recent additions of tattoos. When we were together, he'd only had one on his shoulder, but now his left arm was littered with them as well as one on his chest.

"Why did you get your birth date tattooed on your chest?" I asked, not wanting to disturb our peaceful moment.

He looked into my eyes as if I was the gift he'd always wanted. His left brow arched as if I should have known the answer already.

"It's not just my birthday." He said. "This day means more to me than that, and I have you to thank for it."

My breath hitches in my throat as he places multiple kisses around my neck. He brushes his plump lips against the soft spot between my collarbone and shoulder. I shiver in delight.

"You're all I wanted for my birthday and all I ever needed."

I pulled away to look into his eyes.

"Then have me."

As if he was waiting for confirmation, he attaches his lips to mine. I wasn't holding back either. I could fight the temptation as much as I wanted, but it will always overpower me. It's frightening how much I crave Reed. His hands caress my thighs as one slips between them. I groan at his deliberate brushes against my clothed labia. Every touch is like static electricity. *I'd underestimated how much he remembers.* I tried to hold in my moans, but the second his finger skimmed over my clit, I lost all control.

"Please."

I'd hardly registered that it was my voice crying out for more.

"Please what?"

He's enjoying this far too much.

"Please, just touch me."

"Where?"

I was getting fed up with his teasing. He either needed to touch me or I will do it myself. He must have sensed I wasn't in the mood for his antics as he drew his hand under the lace garment and touched me where I was craving him most. We never broke our eye contact as his fingers traced circles on my clit. He looks at me with lust-glazed eyes as he takes in every twitch or groan from my body, as if he was trying to remember which angles maximized my pleasure. My thighs quivered from the sensational movements of his fingers.

Until the pleasure disappeared.

I hadn't noticed I'd closed my eyes until they shot open in desperation, wanting for the pleasure to return. I watched as he unzipped his pants and my stomach clenched in desire for what lay beneath. The wall supports me as my legs feel like those of a baby deer learning to walk for the first time.

I couldn't wait any longer.

He looked at me from under his lashes as I strode towards him. I place my hands on his chest with a light push. He walked backward to the bed, understanding my intent. I straddle his legs as I trail my fingers up his legs and along his engorged phallus. He thrusts against my hand, but I pulled away.

"You're killing me, Olive."

The nickname sounded different this time. It sent chills of pleasure instead of its usual distaste. I brushed harder to ignite more moans as I craved to hear him call me *Olive* again.

"I've missed this so much." He said. "I can't wait a second longer to be inside you. To fuck you the only way *I* can."

His words alone already had my toes curling. I don't speak a word as I slide the last shred of clothing restricting us, reaching over for the pack of condoms I keep on my bedside table. I could sense he wanted to ask me about it, but his lust clouded his curiosity. He unwrapped the condom, as neither of us could endure the foreplay. He had my legs spread as if it were a marathon, but I was as eager as him.

It's been far too long.

His lips moved against mine with an unparalleled passion. I placed my hand on his chest. Our hearts pounded against our ribcage in perfect harmony, as if they would follow each other's rhythm for eternity. His tip brushed against my clit, causing me to spread my legs further as I groaned at the feeling.

"Are you sure you want to do this?"

He leans further down to lock eyes, as if searching for a hint of hesitancy. *He will not find it.*

"I'm sure."

With the seal of approval, he'd let all worries melt away as our lips reunited. I didn't waste a second in deepening it, having forgotten the effect his simple kisses had on me. I'd been so entranced by his lips that I barely acknowledged his movements until he was spreading my folds. Every inch he moved further was like little bolts of static electricity down my spine. My nails dug into the back of his shoulders as he thrust his hips in a gentle rhythm. I could sense he was trying to restrain himself from going faster, but what would you expect after a year of pent-up sexual tension?

"Don't hold back."

I smile in satisfaction as he shivers, but it's short-lived as he speeds up his thrusts, igniting a groan as I wrap my legs around his waist, increasing the pleasure.

"I've missed hearing your moans." His voice is strained, as if he's biting back moans of his own. "I've missed the way you feel around me."

He'd pulled back to look into my eyes before reaching between us to brush his fingers along my clit. The added sensation almost caused me to scream in ecstasy, but I held it back. Luckily, the music outside would drown out the whimpers. *As well as the creaking of the bed.* My legs twitched as my stomach tightened. I was a quivering mess under his sweltering body. My brain was as crumbled up as the dead leaves of fall.

"Just let go."

His warm breath against my skin added another element of pleasure. His fingers slithered up my thighs, over the juncture of my hips, before settling on my breasts. I draw in a deep breath as he grips them, never faltering with his thrusts. His lips find mine once more and his thumbs circle around my nipples. He knew where to touch me.

"Reed," I said against his lips. "Please."

He also knew how to piss me off.

He halts all his movements, placing his own release on hold for a momentary opportunity to frustrate me.

"Please, what?"

The back of my neck felt hot to the touch, not because I was so close to release, but because of the fury that his conceited grin had ignited.

"What is your problem?"

"I just asked a question."

Frustrated by his untimely jokes, I thrust my hips. He groans at the unexpected movements as his arms buckle, but he regains his composure in the nick of time.

I could sense he wanted to get the upper hand again, but I would not give it up. I trailed my nails along his chest before gripping the back of his neck. The moment I captured his bottom lip between my teeth, I gained the upper hand. He gripped my hips before taking over.

"I can never win."

His voice is strained from his near release, but I was so close I could scarcely speak. His thrusts lost rhythm as my stomach burned like a match had been lit inside of it. I couldn't hold back any longer before I was crying out his name. It was enough for his orgasm to follow mine as our groans of pleasure synced.

Our bated breaths mixed as we took a moment to compose ourselves. He collapsed beside me before rolling off the bed. I don't tear my gaze away from my ceiling, but I can hear him shuffling around. I wanted to get up and redress, but my legs were like gelatin. The bed creaked under his weight as he returned to his spot beside me. I clasp my hands together and place them on my stomach.

"Best birthday ever."

I bite my lip as I think back to those very words uttered a year ago. We were in the exact position, except our situation was different. We're stuck in repetitive purgatory. I had so many questions for him, but I couldn't seem to muster the courage to ask him. However, it seemed fate was advising me against it as someone knocked on my bedroom door.

"Olivia," Penelope's voice called from the outside. "I need my sunflower dress back. Can I come inside?"

Reed

We froze when Penelope tried to turn the door handle after she received no reply from Olivia. It seems my brain wasn't the only one to shut off. Penelope couldn't have chosen a worse time for an outfit change as we were both stark naked above Olivia's sheets.

I was shitting bricks at this point. If she finds us in this predicament, then she'd blab to Marcus. *Which would be the end of me.* I tap the side of her leg to get her attention. *Talk.* I mouth to her.

"I just need a second."

She calls out as we rush off her bed to gather our clothing. I slip my briefs on before I'm being shoved toward the window. I glare at Olivia over my shoulder.

"What are you doing?"

"You need to get out of here."

"Through the window?"

She stops shoving me as she bites off a grin.

"It wouldn't be the first time."

I think back to one of the worst decisions I'd ever made. Perhaps this would be my opportunity to rectify the mistake. *If I don't fall off the roof this time, I will consider it a win.*

"Fine," I said. "It's better than getting caught."

She doesn't give me time to change, as the top half of my body is already leaning out the window. Penelope's knocking becomes more frantic, forcing me to launch myself onto the roof with the rest of my clothes clutched against my chest.

I glance at the party of people hanging around outside, hoping it's too dark for them to find me lurking above them. I tiptoed across the roof towards my bedroom window, not wanting a repeat of the last time I attempted this.

Last summer, I was running away from being caught by Marcus. I didn't pay attention to where I was going; I stubbed my toe before losing my footing. I rolled along the slanted roof before pummeling into Mrs. Huxley's rose bush. We spent the entire night digging thorns out of my skin as everyone interrogated me about why I was on the roof. I diverted their attention onto Connor as he'd done something idiotic that same night, leaving me in the clear.

History better not repeat itself.

I reached the backyard roof, where a few people were lounging by the pool. My bedroom is only a short distance away.

"Someone's on the roof!"

Well, shit.

I watched as some moved back to catch another sight of me, but the darkness swallowed me against the wall, away from the outdoor lights. I take a deep breath before bolting to my bedroom window. I redressed before launching onto my bed, hoping to look casual. The sound of approaching footsteps thump in my ears. I reach for the phone I'd discarded on my bedside table and pretend to be scrolling through *TikTok*. Marcus knocks on my open door. I looked up as if I weren't expecting him.

"I was wondering where you ran off to."

He walks into my room and collapses onto my bed as he gazes up at the ceiling. His arms are by his side. He breathes out through his mouth as he sinks his fingers into his hair.

"Did you hear there was someone on the roof?"

I freeze, but I relax my muscles in hopes of not looking too guilty. I don't look in his eyes; I keep my gaze on the ceiling.

"I guess they wanted to be as cool as me."

"Well, this person didn't fall off the roof." He said. "They're already a step up on you."

I had to bite my tongue to reveal the truth.

"Why are you hiding in my room?"

I was hoping to change the subject.

"I was going to ask you the same thing."

I place my arms behind my head.

"I just needed a breather."

He says nothing as we gaze up at the ceiling as if it were a golden masterpiece instead of a mundane white. The walls are rattling from the intense thumping of the music from downstairs. I tap my fingers against my arm in rhythm with the current song.

"Are you okay?"

It was a loaded question, but also unexpected.

"What do you mean?"

"You haven't been yourself."

I thought I'd fooled everyone into thinking everything was okay. *Marcus isn't just anyone.* I remind myself. He knows me better than anyone; me included.

With one exception.

"I've just been tired, I guess." I said. "It was a stressful year."

And it was. I'd spent the entire time focusing on hockey, that I barely got a moment to catch my breath. And, when I wasn't playing hockey, I attended any party and ended the night with random hookups.

Anything for a distraction. From her.

I was at my loneliest. I'd lost the only girl I'd ever loved, and I could never talk to anyone about it. The guilt I faced every second I looked at Marcus ate me up. It didn't help that he was always a constant reminder of her.

"I'm worried about you." He said. "You were just getting back to a good place."

His concerns are reasonable. I'd spent an entire year on a self-sabotage warpath, but it's as if the moment I saw Olivia again I'd recovered. She was the cure.

"I promised you it would never happen again." I said. "Lesson learned."

He seems pleased with my answer, as he doesn't press the issue.

"We better get back and honor you."

"You do it every day." I said, as I stretched my arms above my head. "You're thankful to have me as your friend."

He snorts.

"Please, it's the other way around."

He bit off a grin.

"Everyone wanted to be my friend. I had other options."

"Charlie Langston doesn't count."

I think back to the memory of the kid who always had a tendency to eat chalk and would blame someone else, saying they stole it. I was often his scapegoat, but I didn't want to dwell on him.

"Let's enjoy the rest of the night."

23

Olivia

Guilt as vast as the ocean had enveloped me, but the pure thrill of what we'd just done gave me strength to keep swimming to the surface. I could only think of one flaw in our reckless actions. He left me wanting more. *Craving* more.

I'm in deep.

A part of me was telling me not to forgive him, not to fall into his trap. The other part of me was telling me to forget the past and enjoy the present. My brain is a walking contradiction.

The first rays of sunlight lit up my room. I could see the fluffy white clouds drifting away with the timid breeze. Despite the promising start to the day, I couldn't seem to get myself out of bed. My mind is spiraling, leaving me incapable of controlling my body to move. I don't know how long I spent in my bed before Chelsea came barging in with her hands on her hips.

"Where did you disappear last night?" She asked.

"Good morning to you, too."

She rolls her eyes but remains in her authoritative stance, like a teacher waiting for you to finish talking so they can finish their lecture. I toss my sheets over my head, but she yanks them off.

"I went for a walk on the beach."

I couldn't look her in the eyes. I'd spent the previous summer lying to her, and I don't think I'd be able to do it again. What kind of person keeps something like this away from their best friend? What kind of sister hooks up with her brother's closest friend?

Different summer, same spiraling thoughts.

"With Wyatt?"

I bit my lip at the mention of his name. He didn't enter my mind the entire time I hooked up with Reed. Even though Wyatt wasn't my boyfriend, I couldn't help but feel like I'd cheated on him. The addition of Wyatt has made my relationship with Reed even more complicated.

It doesn't help that I have so many unasked questions, too.

"No, by myself."

She purses her lips with narrowed eyes before shrugging. She motions for me to move up and slides in next to me.

"I say we have a best friend day." She said. "Away from boys and their drama."

I turn my head.

"Axel problems?"

"He's upset with Reed, and so am I."

I wanted to tell her what I'd heard about the situation and about the things Axel said, but I feared upsetting her. However, it would be wrong of me not to warn her.

"There is something I need to tell you," I said, taking a deep breath. "About Axel."

Her forehead crinkles.

"What do you mean?"

"He said some stuff that annoyed Reed," I said. "That's why he punched him."

"What did he say?"

I brace myself for the imminent confrontation.

"He made comments about sleeping with you and then dumping you."

She gazes across the room at my aged-out poster of *Chad Michael Murray*. I wasn't sure if she was processing the new information or if she didn't believe me.

"I find it hard to believe Reed defended me."

"I wouldn't lie to you."

"I know, but whoever told you this information is not reliable." She narrows her eyes at me. "*Who* told you this information?"

I shrug.

"That's not important, but I just wanted to let you in on what I heard."

She wraps her arm around my waist in a side hug.

"I love you for looking out for me, but I promise I can take care of myself."

I nod my head, knowing I've done all I could. Only time will tell what drama ensues next.

The water is tranquil and undisturbed as I float above the surface. I gaze up at the darkened sky as the stars wink at me from above. The beautiful sight was a contrast to my ugly turmoil. So much has gone on in such a short amount of time and I'm struggling to hold my breath.

I was hoping some alone time in the pool would be the remedy, but it seems as if stress is an incurable indisposition. I've been so concerned about everyone else's business that I'd neglected my own issues at hand.

How am I supposed to choose between the guy that had broken my heart, or the guy that doesn't want it in the first place?

I dive under the water, hoping it will wash away my uncertainties, but it only drenches me further in doubt. I gasp as arms wrap around me. How had I not noticed someone else?

"I've got you alone."

Reed's warm breath ignites a flurry of goosebumps down my spine. I hated how easily my body responded to his presence. I wanted to fight it. Fight him.

"I didn't want anyone disturbing me."

The water ripples as we float to the edge. I wanted to get out, but his tightened hold on my waist restricts me. I make one more attempt before sighing.

"Let me go, Reed."

"Never."

I turn to look at him over my shoulder. He trails kisses down my exposed neck. I gulp before turning around to look into his eyes. He turned his corner lip in an arrogant grin.

"What are you smiling about?"

He trails his fingers down my shoulder and down the strap of my swimsuit. I shivered.

"I've forgotten how easy it is to turn you on."

His words angered me, implying he had some kind of control over me. I placed my hands on his shoulders and shoved him.

"This isn't some kind of game, Reed."

"Isn't it?"

He inches closer to me like a shark to its prey.

"You're a fucking asshole."

The corner of his lip twitches.

"You always knew what to do with that mouth of yours."

His fingers dance along the edge of my thighs.

"Bite your tongue, Reed. You were never good at using it, anyway."

"How would you know?" He asked. "I'm the only guy you've ever been with."

I hated his satisfied smile, and I would do anything to wipe it off.

"Not anymore."

I gave a half-shrug as the arrogance drained from his face. I'd gotten the upper hand and there's nothing he can do about it. My words are pure fabrication, but I couldn't care less.

"You're bluffing."

I puff my chest out and push my shoulders back, feeling far too smug.

"I don't care if you believe me," I said. "Just know he fucked me better than you ever did."

The sinister look in his eyes was evidence that I'd gone too far.

Reed

My nostrils flared as I stared at Olivia. Her slip of the tongue was enough for me to erupt. She'd had sex with *him*. The thought of him making love to her made my blood stir. He didn't deserve her. He wouldn't *love* her.

Not like me.

I wanted to kill him for even being in the same vicinity as her, but my brain had other ideas. To show her how he could never compare. That I'm the only one for her.

"Well, I'm about to make you forget all about him."

"I hate you."

I wrap her legs around my waist, holding her flush against me. I smirk knowing my arrogant grin would set her off even more. *Fuck. She's sexy when she's mad.* I lean closer until our noses brush.

"If this is you hating me, I'm excited to find out what it's like when you love me."

"Fuck you, Adler."

I chuckled and leaned to whisper in her ear.

"That's what you're about to do, Olive."

I could see the lust clouding her eyes, no matter how she tried to hide it. My eyes fall on her parted lips as I trail my fingers up her leg.

Despite the freezing temperatures of the swimming pool, my body is on fire. I press myself flush against her as I trail my finger down her stomach. She sucks it in with a harsh breath. My movements never cease until I reach my destination. She groans as my finger brushes against her clit. I place my other hand over her mouth and lean to whisper in her ear.

"Be quiet, darling," I said. "You wouldn't want to wake everyone up and let them see what I'm doing to you, do you?"

She shakes her head, followed by heavy breaths as I continue to circle my finger along her clit. She clenches her thighs and leans her head against my shoulder.

"I bet he could never make you feel this good."

She mumbles and nods her head.

"Say it," I said as I sped up my movements. "I want to hear you say it."

"He could never make me feel this good."

Her declaration is almost enough to get me off.

"That's my good girl."

I slide her bikini bottoms to the side, placing more pressure on her clit. My eyes fall on her chest as it rises and falls from pleasure. Every whimper is like a shock of gratification to my penis.

She thrusts her chest out as I place kisses above her swimsuit top. Her hips thrust against my hand, eager for more friction. Our eye contact deepens as she spreads her legs, granting me more access. Her eyelids fluttered as she moaned my name.

"I bet St. James never made you feel this good."

Her head falls back.

"Reed, *please.*"

"Please, what?"

I grip her chin, forcing her to look into my eyes.

"I need you to fuck me."

I almost came from her desperation.

"You know I can never say no to you."

I slide my shorts down and grip my rigid length in my hand, teasing her outer lips.

"Stop teasing."

We gasp in unison as I'm enveloped by her. She locks her legs behind me, matching my thrusts. I groan as her nails rake down my spine.

I dig my fingers into her hips as I pick up my pace. Her forehead falls on mine as we exhale in sync. She bites my bottom lip as she clenches around me. I couldn't get enough.

"Turn around." I said into her ear.

She obeys my command, turning around and placing her hands on the edge. She bends further, glancing over her shoulder at me with squinted eyes. I grip her hips before sliding through her folds, groaning at the appetizing new angle. She pushed back against me as I gripped her hair in my hands. She always loved it when I did that.

"You'll forget all about that asshole once I'm done with you," I said. "No one can ever fuck you like me."

I placed kisses on the back of her neck, urging her to let all her inhibitions go. Sliding along her waist, I cast my fingers over her torso and reached over to cup her breasts to help speed up my thrusts. She arches her head back and moans my name louder than intended.

It was enough to set us off. I slouched against her back as our heavy breathing disrupted the calm night. I cocooned her in my arms as I placed tender kisses on top of her head.

"I love you."

My body turns to ice. All color drains from my face. It had been forever since I'd heard them, and I hadn't realized how much I craved hearing those words escape her lips again.

Stay away from her.

The dreaded voice recalled. I close my eyes and shake the thoughts away, but they fight back.

You're only going to drag her down with you.

I think back to the confrontation, the one that ended it all. The poison to our love. The extinguisher. All I had to do was embrace her. To lean forward and attach my lips to hers. To show her the unquenchable love and desire I feel for her.

But I'm an idiot.

"I have to go."

I couldn't look back as I hoisted myself out of the pool. The grief-stricken look on her face would kill me, especially since I'm the one that caused it. I know I'm making the biggest mistake, but it's too late to go back now.

Olivia

I've often returned to the beach for solace, as if the waves were the crystal ball of answers. I'd been struggling with my erratic thoughts and hesitation. Despite the infuriating alarm bells in my mind warning me to stay clear of Reed, I couldn't help but gravitate towards him. He always had a charismatic aura that had people vying for something as simple as his acknowledgment.

Especially me.

I breathe in the salty air as I close my eyes, allowing myself to pretend I was floating away in the ocean. Away from all my worries.

"It seems you needed an escape, too."

I nearly lost my balance, but I dug my hands in the sand. Brynlee looks at me.

"Too bad it's only temporary."

She makes herself comfortable beside me as she leans back on her elbows.

"Love drama?" I can only nod. "What did Reed do now?"

"We hooked up."

My eyes widened at how easily I confessed to her, but despite the brief interactions I've had with her, I've learned she's easy to talk to.

"I did not expect that." She said. "Actually, I did."

"You did?"

She chuckles.

"I could sense the sexual tension from miles away."

I tuck my legs in and fold my arms around my knees. Could she sense it because she's the only one who knows about mine and Reed's history? Or is it because she's observant?

"Look, I didn't want to ask, but I think knowing might help." She said. "What happened between you and Reed?"

What didn't happen?

I scrunch my nose as I clutch my knees tighter. Am I willing to relive the devastating memories? I'd never spoken about it aloud before. I'd kept it in a vault, hoping it would never get out.

Maybe it's time it did.

"Near the end of last summer, I got sick," I said. "I had leukemia as a kid, and it came back."

She sits upright and faces me, but she doesn't speak a word. Her eyes plead for me to continue.

"I spent my entire senior year in and out of the hospital." I take a deep breath. "However, near the end of last summer, I got worse. The doctors didn't think I was going to make it."

I hadn't realized I started crying until a teardrop fell on my leg. My heart feels heavy as I relive the trauma I'd tried so hard to bury.

"My parents took me from doctor to doctor for another opinion, but they were all the same." I wipe my cheeks. "They didn't think I would even make graduation."

She places a comforting hand on mine.

"Reed and I were a secret, so he had to visit me when my parents were gone," I said. "He always supported me, ensuring that my pillows were fluffed, or that I had enough blankets."

I noticed a river of tears flowing down her face.

"Yet, no matter how strong he tried to be for me, I knew it was too much for him to handle," I said. "He was a college freshman, he should have been out partying, not taking care of his sick girlfriend, who was going to die, anyway."

My voice cracks at the end. I take deep breaths to compose myself, however, retelling the story floods me with misery.

"A few weeks later, I got the amazing news that my new treatment worked," I said. "The doctors said it was miraculous."

I tuck away the strands of hair stuck to my soaked cheeks.

"I couldn't wait to tell Reed the news, but I never saw him again," I said. "Not until this summer."

She gasps and places her hand over her mouth.

"He just left?" I nod my head. "Why have you never confronted him?"

I shrug.

"I guess I was afraid of the answer."

She moves closer to me and wraps her arms around my shoulder as I sob into her chest. My body shakes as all the suppressed emotions erupt, like a volcano coming out of dormancy.

"As much as you're afraid of the answer, I think you owe it to yourself to find out." She said. "It's the missing piece for you to make your decision."

I furrow my brows.

"What decision?"

"If you can forgive him or move on without him."

24

Reed

I swung my hockey stick against the puck with brute force, allowing my anger to flow into the net. I don't know why I'm fuming. Wait, that's a lie. I'm pissed off because Olivia has been avoiding me for days. If she entered the same room as me, she'd reroute to another. I did not know it was possible to avoid someone you're living with, but she's succeeded.

I just wish she'd talk to me.

I know I fucked up. I just don't know how to fix it.

I slam another puck into the net before dropping the stick in frustration. Hockey helps release the pent-up anger, but every time I hit the puck away, thoughts of Olivia return to mind.

"Marcus told me I'd find you here."

Connor's voice echoes throughout the arena. I take off my helmet and skate to the edge to join him.

"Why were you looking for me?"

I take a seat on the steps and loosen my skates.

"I just wanted to check up on you. You haven't been yourself."

Connor has never been observant, so for him to notice means I haven't been fooling anyone.

"I've just had a lot on my mind."

He nods his head and hums in agreement before taking a seat next to me.

"My sister is messing with your head, isn't she?"

I freeze and my jaw feels slack. My laces slipped from my fingers as my skates clattered to the ground.

"What are you talking about?"

He chuckles and delivers a harsh pat on my back.

"Let's not pretend you haven't been sneaking around with her."

His tone holds no anger. He's as casual as if we were discussing dinner options.

"How did you find out?"

He chuckles and folds his arms across his chest, like a smug detective who just solved the case.

"It wasn't hard to figure out when I saw you climb out her window stark naked."

My brows furrow as I think back to the night of my birthday party. I at least had my briefs on.

"I wasn't naked that night."

"I'm talking about last summer."

Once again, it felt like my heart was going to take off out of my chest.

He's known since last summer.

"Why did you say nothing?"

"I figured you'd talk when you were ready." He said. "It was never my secret to tell."

I turn to look at Connor, *really* look at him. When did the immature little boy become so wise? I used to see him as the rebellious little brother who made his own rules, but now I'm seeing him in a new light.

It's like he'd morphed his entire personality over the summer.

"Thank you."

I mean it. If he'd snitched on us last summer, then everything would have changed. We were never ready to spill our secret, or I was never ready. I'd always been so afraid of losing Marcus that I never realized I would lose Olivia. And now, my own fears and insecurities are making me lose her again.

"It's her birthday tomorrow," Connor said. "She may not admit it, but I know she wants you there."

Her birthday is eight days after mine, and it was always a call for celebration. However, it was just a few days after her birthday last year that everything went downhill.

He taps my shoulder before standing up and strutting out of the arena. Once he's out of sight, I reach into my bag and dig around until my hands grasp the rectangular purple box. I open it up to look at the Galaxy necklace. It looks like Saturn with a ring of stars around it.

I found it months ago in a store near campus. I thought of Olivia the moment I saw it and bought it. It's been burning a hole in my bag ever since. I could never muster the courage to give it to her, but maybe her birthday is the perfect time.

Maybe this was all worth the wait.

Olivia

Ever since I'd gotten sick, my birthday has been an even bigger celebration than normal. It's no longer just about the day I was born, but also a celebration of my survival. Every year is like a miracle for my family and for me.

I woke up to more chatter than usual, more voices. With furrowed brows, I toss my sheets to the side before speed-walking downstairs. The voices became more distinct, but I feared my ears were deceiving me. The moment I stepped into the kitchen, I gasped as I noticed my parents and my oldest brother, Eli, standing around the counter with a cup of coffee in their hands. They all turned to me with wide smiles.

"Happy Birthday!"

I reach Eli first as he wraps his arms around me, lifting me off the ground. I fought the urge to cry, but my emotions were overpowering.

"Happy Birthday, little sis." He whispered in my ear.

I embraced my parents next, not having expected them to come all the way, not after how tense everything was before we left for the beach house.

"I'm so happy you're all here." I said as I wiped away the fallen tears.

"You know we'd never miss this day."

Eli ruffled my hair. I roll my eyes at his usual annoying antics. The sound of a party horn vibrates in my ear as Connor comes bustling in. He's got a party hat on his head, which he takes off to place on mine.

"Happy Birthday!"

He cheers before pulling me into a bone-crushing hug.

After another round of hugs and wishes from Marcus, Penelope, and Chelsea, I seek solace in my bedroom to prepare myself for the day.

Penelope, Chelsea, and my mom insisted on taking me out for a *girl's day,* but I know that's their way of distracting me so my brothers and dad could set up for my birthday party. They do it every year as if the outcome would be different, but I always play along.

We were going to spend the morning at the country club and have a relaxing day by the pool, which couldn't have come at a better time. I need some serious *R&R.*

"Are you ready, birthday girl?"

Chelsea stands in the doorway with her sky-blue sundress, a contrast to my black one.

"I am now."

I smile before linking my arms with hers as we skip down the stairs to enjoy the beautiful summer's day.

We were greeted with the delighted squeals of the kids splashing each other in the swimming pool, along with the lifeguard yelling for them to stop. I chuckle as they continue to defy his orders. One boy even dunks another boy's head under the water as another cannonballs beside them drenching the lifeguard standing at the edge.

We find a spot with recliners to spend a moment basking in the sun's rays. I, however, found a comfortable spot under the umbrella. Sunshine is not my friend. I glance around the area as my mom rants about our neighbors back home, whose leaves keep getting blown over to our side. I roll my eyes at her dramatic narration.

I glance around, hoping to find something to distract myself.

A pair of lifeguards piqued my attention, chatting near the pool, but one seemed familiar. My eyes widened in delight as she turned around.

"Brynlee!" I called, jumping from my spot to approach her.

She turns at the call of her name and offers me a wide grin.

"Hey, Olivia."

"I had no idea you were a lifeguard."

She glances down at her signature red swimsuit and whistle necklace.

"What gave it away?"

I chuckle before looking over my shoulder to find my mom still talking their ear off. An idea enters my mind.

"It's my birthday today."

"Happy Birthday!" She said, before wrapping her arms around my shoulders.

She pulls out of the hug with a wide grin.

"My family is throwing me a surprise party, and I was hoping you'd come."

"It's not much of a surprise if you know about it."

"My family isn't subtle."

The corner of her lips rises.

"In that case, I'd love to come."

I was happy with her acceptance. There's something about Brynlee that makes you feel at ease just by talking to her. We talked for a while about her job and her majoring in marine biology. Our shared love for animals made me like her even more. I noticed my mom was at the bar, so I took it as my queue to return to Penelope and Chelsea.

"I'll see you later." I said, before walking back to spend time with my unsuspecting family.

25

Reed

Olivia's family had set up everything for the surprise party half an hour ago. The tradition is always for her family to surprise her before the guests arrive. It's always some random friends Connor makes over the summer.

He could make friends with a palm tree.

However, it's not much of a surprise. I know Olivia. She's always been the worst at hiding her surprise, or maybe I'm just so good at reading her. I was hiding outside on the back porch, trying to avoid Mr. Huxley. He's never been my biggest fan.

I've been nursing my can of *White Claw* for the past twenty minutes as I gaze out into the nightly abyss. I saw a figure pacing back and forth just outside on the beach. It looked as if they were about to approach the house before turning around. They repeated this cycle until I got annoyed and approached them. I regretted it as I got closer to them. The moonlight reflected on his face, and I scrunched my nose in disgust.

St. James.

"What's your problem?" I asked, before taking a large gulp of my drink.

"I never even knew it was Olivia's birthday." He said. He was in such a state of panic that I don't think he registered who he was talking to. "What am I going to do?"

I wanted to tell him to get lost, to just go home and cut his losses. I wanted to tell him to forget Olivia and move on.

I couldn't.

Olivia likes him, and I can't be selfish. Despite everything, I would do anything to keep her happy.

I love her, and I never want to cause her any pain.

I reach into my pocket and hold my hand inside after a moment's hesitation, before extending the gift to him. He looks at it as if something is about to jump out and bite him. I roll my eyes and shove it into his hand.

"Give this to her." He opens the box to reveal the Galaxy necklace. "She'll love it. And you."

His brows furrow.

"Why are you helping me?"

Is he that dense?

"She cares about you, and contrary to popular belief, I care about her."

He looks at the jewelry in his hand, inspecting it as if he were a jeweler.

"You're in love with her, aren't you?"

This is too unusual for me. Who would have ever thought that I would engage in a civilized conversation with Wyatt St. James?

"You, of all people, should know how easy it is to fall in love with her."

He glances at the necklace before closing the box. He places it in the pocket of his hoodie.

"Well, thank you."

As if he's still trying to process all of this. He walks past me to go inside the house, but I grab his arm before he can get any further.

"Treat her right," I said, almost pleading. "She's the girl you will regret losing."

He nods his head. I watched as he walked towards the home, but I couldn't find the desire to follow. I cannot find the strength to watch the girl I love fall in love with someone else.

"Where do you think you're going?"

A voice called as I ventured toward the beach.

"I'm not in the mood, Brynlee."

I don't turn around. I keep strutting to the beach, but I can hear her footsteps echoing mine. I roll my eyes as she picks up pace until she's at my side. We don't speak until we're close to the water.

"Why did you do that?"

"Do what?"

"Give him your gift."

"I don't know what you're talking about."

She nudges my shoulder with hers.

"Why do you always have to pretend you're not capable of doing nice things?"

I glance at her from the corner of my eye.

"Because, if you always do nice things, people always expect it," I said. "I'm not a good person, so I'm just going to end up disappointing."

I don't know what reaction I expected her to have, but laughing at my confession wasn't even on the list.

"Do you think I would have spent so much time hanging out with you if you were a bad person?" She asked. "You underestimate yourself, Adler."

My shoulders slouch and I slide my fingers through my hair.

"She's better off without me," I said, craning my neck to the sky. "What's the point of doing good when you lose the ones you love, regardless?"

She places her hand on my knee.

"You didn't lose her because of that." She said. "You lost her because you're an idiot."

Her words were a massive reality check. As if it was the sucker punch I needed to get my mind thinking again.

I haven't.

She told me she loved me. After everything I did, she still loved me. All I had to do was tell her I felt the same.

I'm an idiot. Just like Brynlee said.

"It would be selfish of me to take her away from someone that makes her happy."

She shakes her head.

"It's selfish that you're pushing her away and not letting her decide what she wants."

I hate that she always knows what to say.

"Do you have any idea how annoying you are?"

Her smug grin says it all.

"You can thank me later." She said. "Let's go get your girl."

Olivia

The moment I stepped into the unlit home; I delivered an *Oscar-worthy* performance. I placed my hand on my chest in mock surprise as they jumped out of their hiding spots, followed by the synchronized *surprise.* I even added some fake tears.

"This is amazing."

It's the truth. Even though there was no surprise, I appreciate the effort they made to celebrate me. For the first time in a long time, I have my family together again. I made the rounds of hugging everyone but stopped in my tracks as Wyatt stood in the background with an anxious smile on his face.

I guess my family surprised me, after all.

"Happy Birthday, gorgeous." He said, embracing me in his arms.

I don't hug him for too long knowing there are dozens of eyes on us, especially my parents, and they have yet to meet him.

I intertwine my fingers with his and direct him to my parents and eldest brother. The look on his face was as if I was about to launch him off a cliff. I couldn't blame him. Eli was staring him down as if he were scrutinizing every inch of him.

"Everyone, this is Wyatt."

He waves as they stare him down. My mom was the first to greet him. She wraps her arms around him in a welcoming embrace.

"I've seen you at a few hockey games." My dad said to him.

Am I the only one who never noticed Wyatt until this summer? To be fair, I never paid attention to hockey, not even when my brothers played.

He and my dad bonded over their shared love for hockey. I was happy to see how well he got on with my parents. The beautiful moment was ruined as Reed entered the room, followed by Brynlee. My mother bolted out of her seat to embrace him.

"I felt like I haven't seen you at all." she said, embracing him in a motherly hug.

Reed was as much her son as her own, which is understandable, considering he's been in our lives for as long as I can remember.

"I've missed you."

As much as I dislike Reed, I cannot deny he loves my mother as much as she does him. He'd always looked up to her.

Especially since he lost his own.

Wyatt clears his throat beside me and intertwines his fingers with mine. He leans down to whisper in my ear.

"Can we go somewhere quieter?"

I nod and lead him outside, feeling claustrophobic from all the eyes caging us in.

We sat on the steps of the porch, but he never made eye contact with me the entire time. He twirls his thumbs as his feet tap the ground.

"I never expected you to become so special to me." He said. "I met you when I'd almost given up on finding love, but I think I'm finding it again. All because of you."

I expected to feel butterflies or to feel as if I was about to float away if he wasn't holding my hand. I'd read hordes of books and analyzed dozens of movies. This is the part where I'm supposed to feel on top of the world. To have my dream guy confess how he feels about me, we'd kiss and then live happily ever after.

But, he isn't my dream guy.

It took this moment for me to realize it. The reality of my feelings came to light. It became more abundant when he reached into his pocket and presented me with a box. He opens it to reveal the most stunning necklace I have ever seen.

Yet, it's too much of a coincidence. How could Wyatt have known what that symbolizes to me?

My stomach clenches as the back of my eyes burns. Acid bubbled up in my gut. He doesn't know the truth, so how could he know about this? The thoughts kept repeating in my mind.

I'd only ever told one person.

My brain shut down to the point where I couldn't move my fingers. I couldn't reach for the extended necklace.

"Are you okay?"

"I'll be right back."

The rising bile burns my throat as my face becomes drenched in perspiration. I didn't stop running until my feet touched the sand of the beach. I leaned forward, placing my hands on my knees as I took generous gulps of air. My legs wobbled.

Why am I in such a state?

Over the noise of the ocean, I could hear the distinct sound of the sand crunching under someone's weight. I wiped my tears, but new ones kept falling.

"You look awful."

Connor jokes as he squishes beside me.

"Thanks."

He leans forward to get a better glimpse of my face, which I attempt to hide with my hair. I feel his arm move around my shoulder as he pulls me closer and I place my head on his shoulder, needing comfort.

"Do you remember when Todd McCain kissed you and then told everyone he kissed a frog?"

Is he trying to make me feel worse?

It was one of the worst memories I've had. I had the biggest crush on him in the second grade. He was a year older and would always hang out with my brother and Reed. I was minding my business in the cafeteria when he approached me and confessed his feelings for me. I had no idea his friends had dared him to do it until he leaned over, kissed me, and proclaimed to the entire cafeteria that the toad hadn't transformed into a princess.

"How could I forget?" I said. "I was so happy later that day when a soccer ball broke his nose."

Connor chuckles.

"He didn't break his nose from getting hit by a soccer ball." He said. I pulled away to look at him in shock. "Reed punched him."

That makes little sense. Reed had told me the details of how they were playing soccer, and some kid kicked a bit too hard.

He lied to me.

"Why would Reed not tell me?"

"He's Reed," Connor said. "He would do things like that all the time."

"What do you mean?"

It's his turn to look at me as if I'm oblivious.

"Do you think that Jamie Hossler glued her *own* hair together?"

I'd always believed it was *karma* that targeted my tormentors, but this entire time, it had been

Reed acting as my guardian angel. He'd been lurking in the shadows, waiting for a moment to sweep in to help me. He fought for me until I learned to fight for myself.

"Why are you telling me all of this?"

"Because," He exhales. "I know you're in love with each other."

I'd forgotten how to breathe. Of all the people I thought would have found out about Reed and me, Connor was the last person on my list. In fact, he wasn't even *on* the list.

"How did you find out?"

I don't have the energy to deny it.

"I always suspected, especially last summer." He said. "My suspicions were confirmed when I saw him sneaking out your bedroom window one night."

I draw my fingers through the sand.

"It doesn't matter," I said. "We're no good for each other."

"I disagree." He said. "I'd never seen you so happy."

"He left me when I needed him the most."

"What he did was wrong." He agrees. "Have you ever wondered if something, or *someone*, influenced his decision?"

"I'm not following."

"The guy loves you more than anything, Olivia." He insisted. "It's hard to believe his feelings could flip like a switch."

I wanted to believe that's the case, to believe in what Reed and I have, but he's given me no reason to trust him.

I was so fixed on my nagging thoughts that I never realized Connor had stood until his outstretched hand was in front of my face.

"We can stress about logistics later." He said. "Tonight is your night and you're missing out on some darn magnificent cake."

As if he'd lifted the ponderous weight of burden off my shoulders, I stand up and wrap my arms around his waist.

"Thank you."

He wraps his arms around my shoulders and squeezes me tight.

"Enough sappy stuff. Let's go have some fun."

26

Reed

I downed my fifth *White Claw* as I watched the train wreck unfolding before me. Mr. Huxley hadn't stopped talking to *St. James* the entire time. It's as if he was hanging on every word, laughing at anything the elder man said.

What a kiss ass.

In desperate need of something stronger, I make a beeline for the kitchen. The guests were arriving and I'm in no mood for conversation. I dug through the cabinets for Mr. Huxley's secret stash of *Bourbon*.

"You won't find it. It's locked away."

I hit my head on the door. Mrs. Huxley stood in the doorway with her arms crossed over her chest. A scolding glare I have been on the receiving end far too often. I close the cabinet and lean back against the counter.

"I was looking for a snack."

She raises her brow at my transparent fabrication.

"You forget I can tell when you're lying." I drop my head. "Is something bothering you?"

She walks further into the room. I shake my head.

"I'm just not in the mood for a crowd."

The explosive arrival of the guests only further proves my statement. I'm in no position to socialize, especially not with a bunch of insipid drunks.

"I hope you're not going back to your old ways."

The statement alone is enough to make me lose my reserve. Everything I've been holding back, everything I've worked so hard on, collapsed in a microsecond. The shelved memories tipped over, feeling as if they shattered my chest, leaving nothing left to protect my heart.

"I don't know."

I couldn't recognize the hollow voice as my own. I could pretend all I wanted with everyone else, but never Mrs. Huxley. She was the mother I had never had.

She wrapped her arms around me in a motherly embrace. It wasn't uncomfortable at all. In fact, it was as if she was trying to radiate every ounce of love for me like the sun with its warmth.

"You're going to be okay."

My arms wrap around her like chains.

"How can you be so certain?"

"I know because I've had the honor of watching you grow into the man you are today." I drenched her shoulder with tears. I pulled away to wipe my tears away, but she beat me to it. "I don't know what's going on with you, but know I love you."

The tears cascade down my face like a waterfall. If I cry any more, we're going to flood the kitchen.

"I messed up."

I choke back a sob. Her hands cup my face, forcing me to look into her eyes.

"That's life." She said. "We all lose ourselves at least once, but finding the courage to find your way back makes everything better."

I square my shoulders and bite the corner of my lip to hold back anymore tears. Her words resonate in my mind. I've been a coward. I'd been so afraid of the feelings I had for Olivia that I let my demons taint the purity of our love. I'd sacrificed definite happiness in fear of potential sadness. *She is worth a thousand more heartbreaks.*

"Greg and I are going to get out of your hair now." Mrs. Huxley interrupts my thoughts. "Please, behave."

She squeezes my hands before exiting the kitchen, leaving me to my entangled thoughts. However, it all accumulated into one.

Go get your girl.

It was enough to ignite the embers of doubt. I bolted through the crowd and out the door I last saw Olivia exiting. I hadn't expected that I would have to scour the entire beach for her. Yet, as fate would have it, she approached the back porch with Connor. She halted after the first step when she saw me standing a few feet away. It's as if she was debating on making a run for it, but Connor stopped her.

"Can we talk?" I asked.

My voice froze. Connor makes the first move by dragging her up the stairs.

"You can't avoid him forever." He said. "You owe this to *yourself.*"

He returns to the party, leaving us alone.

"You have five minutes." She said with open disdain.

I wracked my brain for the perfect thing to say. For the perfect explanation. However, there's no excuse for what I'd done.

She could never know the truth.

Time was running out and my lack of response was angering her, so I said the first thing that popped into my mind.

"I love you."

The thin line of her brow jumped in surprise. She reeled in astonishment.

"Excuse me?"

"I love you."

Her face grew ashen as she shook her head.

"Stop fucking around, Reed."

I take a step forward to gauge her reaction. She doesn't flinch, giving me the confidence to step closer to her.

"This isn't a game."

She covers her face with her hands before drawing her fingers through her hair. She grips her roots.

"You don't love me."

"I do."

"You don't hurt the ones you love."

"That's *bullshit*," I said. "The ones you love are the ones that can hurt you the most. I made a mistake and I'm trying to rectify it."

"Why now?" She asked, losing patience. "Why, after all this time? Is it because I'm no longer sick?"

That statement was like a stake to the heart. Is this the person she believed me to be?

"That's not fair." I said. "I didn't leave because you were sick."

"You could have fooled me." She said. "I needed you and you were gone."

"It wasn't because you were sick."

"Then tell me why!"

If it wasn't for the abrasive music inside, we would have gathered an unwanted audience. Each word we speak becomes higher.

"I can't do that!"

This time I was the one getting fed up. Annoyed. Annoyed with myself because I knew I could never tell her the truth.

It would kill her.

"I am done with this conversation."

She shoves her shoulder against mine, but I keep a firm grip on her wrist.

"I'm *sorry.*"

She pulls from my hold, gazing at me with an unfamiliar hatred.

"I'm sorry for ever allowing myself to fall in love with you."

She walked closer and pointed an accusatory finger at my chest. I was the one to pull away this time.

"How could you say that?"

She chuckled.

"I thought I was going to die." She said. "I thought those were my last moments, and all I wanted was you. To hold you. To kiss you. To tell you how much I loved you for the last time."

The tears glide down her cheeks. My vision of her became blinded by tears of my own.

"I wanted you to be the last person I saw before it was all over, and you weren't there." She said. "I wanted to tell you I love you one more time."

Her words knocked me back to reality. I'd never taken her feelings into consideration. I almost lost her. But I *need* her to know how I feel.

"We all suffered alongside you, Olivia. The moment you got sick again, my entire life turned upside down because I had to imagine a world without you in it. Do you know how difficult that is to do when my entire world is with you?"

She shakes her head in disbelief.

"I don't believe you."

I step closer to her, wanting her to understand the severity of my words. To know how much I love her.

"We're perfect for each other, Olivia. You can't deny that."

She shakes her head.

"Maybe we are, but that doesn't mean we're meant to be." She said. "I'm sorry, but you had your chance last summer, and you blew it."

I drop my head to hide the rising tears.

"Wyatt is in there waiting for me. I owe it to him and us to give our relationship a chance." She said. "You will always be my first love, Reed, but that doesn't mean you're my last."

"I'm not," I said. "I'm your forever. We both know it."

Her eyes brim with tears.

"You're my everything, Olivia." I approached her. "I thought giving you time to heal would be best for you, but I was wrong. We just needed each other. I don't want to spend another second without you knowing how endless my love for you is."

She began mumbling to herself. I strained my ears to hear, but I only caught a few words.

Fuck it.

I gasped into her mouth as her lips attached to mine. I slithered my hands down her back to grip her waist. One kiss was enough to fix every insecurity or doubt I had in my mind. She's always been my remedy.

"What the *fuck* is going on here?"

We pulled away. We were so entrapped by each other that we hadn't noticed the music stopped and an audience gathered in the doorway.

Marcus got a front-row view.

"I can explain." I said, but closed my mouth as he pointed a finger in my direction.

"*You* don't get to speak right now." Penelope places a hand on his shoulder to calm him, but he shrugs her off. "How long has this been going on?"

Neither of us spoke, knowing any answer would enrage him.

"I think we should all calm down."

Eli steps in.

"This has nothing to do with you." Marcus said. "You're gone most of the time, leaving me to deal with all of this, so let me do it."

Marcus' anger towards us was reflected right into Eli. It became a stare-down of brothers.

"Stop it, both of you."

Olivia spoke as tears cascaded down her eyes. I raised my hand to wipe them away, but Marcus' resenting voice stopped me.

"*Don't* touch her."

Connor holds him back from launching his fist into my face.

"Calm down, Marcus." He said. "It's not that big of a deal."

He breaks from Connor's grip and shoves him with so much force he tumbles back into Eli.

"Not a big deal?" Marcus scoffs. "He's the reason she was crying her eyes out every night for months!" He glared at me with such fury. His eyes were scorching like gasoline to a flame. "I trusted you. I told you about how hurt she was over some guy and this entire time it was you!"

He launched for me again, but Olivia stepped between us.

"Stop it!" She said. "Can't we talk about this?"

"No!" Marcus screams before bolting past her.

I barely had time to react before his fist collided with my cheek, and I lost my balance with the unexpected impact. I hit the ground with a thud before clutching my blood-covered cheek.

My body ignited with fury as I launched off the ground and tackled him to the floor. We rolled around like a haystack in the wind until Connor screamed Olivia's name. Everyone rushed towards her. I pulled away from Marcus and looked over my shoulder at the crowd. Through the gap between their feet, I see Olivia unconscious on the ground.

❀

It all feels like a fever dream. It's almost been a year since we were last in this position. The smell of pine and antiseptic nauseates me. The hallway felt like we were sucked into a black hole filled with infinite twists and turns.

A television played in the corner as I slouched further in the uncomfortable seats. An elderly lady hacked and coughed on the other side of the room. I placed my head in my hands to hide from the tense atmosphere. The waiting room was spacious, but I still felt claustrophobic. It's as if Marcus' glare was choking me. The ticking of the clock was fucking with my mind. The wait is killing me. None of us has heard anything about Olivia.

It's like last year all over again.

A lady walked in with her newborn baby wrapped in a fleece blanket. The shrill wail echoes throughout the room and into the hallway. I'm sure people in the other ward could hear the cries. Its face turned as red as a tomato, but the screams never wavered.

I almost knocked the chair to the ground due to how quickly I stood up, brushing past everyone in the hallway, not caring if I caused a scene. I didn't stop until I reached the exit and the crisp air wafted through my nostrils, as if I'd been holding my breath. My hands fell to my knees as the tears flooded my face.

I might lose her. For real, this time.

I sit on the top step and drop my head between my legs, struggling to breathe. I close my eyes and clutch the fabric of my shirt above my heart. It takes a few meditated inhales to calm me down.

I feel a presence sitting next to me. Marcus doesn't speak as he gazes out into the parking lot with his arms leaning on his knees. We watched as cars entered and exited for what felt like hours before he spoke.

"What the *fuck*, Reed?" He said and turned to look at me. "You and my sister?"

There's an incessant throb in my heart as I think back to the look of betrayal on his face when he heard my confession to Olivia. I fucked up, and it's up to me to make it right. I needed to explain myself.

"When my parents died, I was so scared. I'd moved to this new town with my uncle having to start my life all over again." I said. "Then I met this kid when he kicked his ball onto our lawn."

He smiles at the memory of the day we met.

"I don't think you know how you saved my life, Marcus," I said, looking up at the sky to hold back the tears. "You saved me from the darkest time in my life. I don't want to imagine what my life would have turned out like if I hadn't met you."

It was his turn to hold back the floodgates.

"And if I hadn't met you, I wouldn't have found Olivia," I said as a lone tear fell down my cheek and pooled at my feet. "I've loved her for the longest time, but I kept denying it, telling myself she's nothing but my best friend's sister, because that guaranteed I'd always have her in my life, and I wouldn't lose you. I don't want to hide it anymore. She's worth losing everything for."

He wipes his face with the back of his hand. He pokes the inside of his cheek with his tongue with a faraway look in his eyes.

"I'm not pissed because you fell in love with her." He said. "I'm hurt you kept it a secret from me."

I bit my lip and dropped my head. The last thing I've ever wanted to do was hurt him.

"You're my brother," I said. "You've always been the most important person in my life until I fell in love with Olivia."

I placed my hand on his back, mustering the courage to look at him.

"I'm sorry I betrayed you. I am. I hope one day you can see the positive influence she has on me and see that I'm becoming a better person because of her."

He stands up and holds out his hand. I gaze at him like a lost child having just found their mother.

"I already do."

I place my hand in his and he hauls me up and into his arms. I wrap mine around him as we both sob on each other's shoulders. Our tears are an accumulation of happiness for reconciling, as well as the fear that we might lose someone that we can't live without.

"I'm sorry I punched you." He said. "We had a deal, though."

I laugh as I think back on our deal. The one where I told him he could punch me in the face if I ever fell in love.

Someone clears their throat, disturbing us from our emotional outlet. Our heads turn to see Mr. Huxley standing with his arms across his chest. He pulls down his eyebrows as if anchors were tugging them.

"Olivia is awake." The words were like an injection of adrenaline. My cheeks rise until they hurt. "Only immediate family may see her."

The rush ended before it could course through my body. He was looking at me as he spoke. Marcus looked at me, silently asking if I'd be okay.

"Don't worry about it," I said. "Please tell her I'm here."

He nods his head and pats my back before rushing through the door. Mr. Huxley stayed behind. His narrowed eyes stared me down. I don't quiver from his attempt at intimidation. We stared each other down as if this was a Western movie and we were about to draw. I opened my mouth to ask what his deal was, but he beat me to it by uttering the words that started this whole mess.

"I thought I told you to stay away from my daughter."

27

Olivia

The pungent smell of disinfectant invaded my nostrils. I opened my eyes, blinking to sharpen my blurred vision. My memory is hazy.

How did I end up here? Has the entire year been a dream, and I'm still sick in the hospital?

The pale blue walls and the beeping of the monitors are like an unpleasant trip. It feels like someone is pounding a hammer against my brain and my mouth is as dry as the *Sahara Desert*. I tried to sit up straighter, but my arms felt like gelatin.

"Be careful."

Eli rushes into the room and helps me to stack the pillows higher. I sigh as my strained muscles loosen. My forehead felt scorching as strands of my hair were stuck to it. He pushed the tattered hairs away as he looked at me with knitted brows.

"What happened?"

It hurt to speak, like sandpaper to my throat.

"You passed out after Marcus and Reed's argument." He said. "You'd been unconscious for a few hours."

The memories flashed in the back of my eyes in intervals until I could remember the entire scene. I could remember how scared I was as I watched my brother and his best friend deliver punches to each other. I remember feeling lightheaded as I pleaded for them to stop until it all faded, like the ending credits of a movie.

"Where are they?"

"They're outside waiting to see you."

I don't know who I dreaded seeing more. The brother I lied to and betrayed, or the boy I love who once ran away before because of this predicament.

"I want to see Marcus."

Eli nods before reaching down to kiss the top of my head and mutters *I love you.* My stomach clenches as Marcus peered his head inside. I chew on my bottom lip as he sits beside the bed. My fingers tingle as my heartbeat pounds against my head.

"What happened to taking it easy?"

"I'm sorry," I said. "I never meant for anyone to get hurt."

He clasps his fingers together as he exhales.

"None of that matters now." He said. "The important thing is that you're okay."

There's a knot in my throat, and I close my eyes until the burning fades.

"I'm scared."

My voice cracks as my fingers tremble at the thought of something being wrong again. His eyes are bloodshot as he wipes his face with the sleeve of his hoodie. His breathing is uneven as he reaches out to squeeze my hand.

"We'll deal with it once we know for certain." He said. "We always do."

I nod as I pick at my nails.

"Are you upset with Reed?"

He draws his hand down his face.

"I was," He said. "Until we talked it out."

"Good."

I didn't know what else to say. I'm prolonging the inevitable conversation.

"I shouldn't make him wait any longer." Marcus said. "He's dug a hole in the hallway from all his pacing."

I attempt a grin as he squeezes my hand once more before walking out of the room. He hardly has time to exit before Reed is pushing past him. He's by my side as quick as *The Flash*.

"How are you feeling?"

"Not the best."

His bottom lip juts out as he places a kiss on my forehead. My face burned, and this time it's not from a fever.

"Is there anything I can get you?"

My heart warms at his characteristic concern and helpfulness. It's been a long time since I've been able to see this side of Reed. It's the only positive I can find through the piles of negativity.

"I just want you to hold me."

There's no hesitation in his movements as he hoists himself onto the bed, making himself comfortable before patting his chest. I peck his cheek before snuggling up against him with my head on his chest. I wrap my arm around his abdomen, inhaling his calming scent. His arms wrap around me, warming me up, as my heartbeat catches up with his.

"I'm sorry." He said.

I tilted my head to look into his eyes.

"For what?"

"For abandoning you last summer." He said. "I'll never forgive myself for doing it."

"At least tell me why." I said. "What made you do it?"

His fingers slide down my arms, igniting an array of goosebumps.

"Please trust me when I say I can't tell you." He said. "I'm doing it to protect you."

I want to trust him, but my desire to know overrules.

"Why can't I know?"

"Olivia, it's better if you don't."

My eyes burned with frustrated tears. I need to know what could have provoked him to abandon everything we had. I'd spent an entire year in doubt.

"Please, just leave."

The words escaped my mouth before I could process them. The concern of not knowing why I'm in hospital, accumulated with the insecurities, was too much for me to handle. I needed a break from everything.

Reed didn't argue. He nodded his head and walked out, leaving me to dwell on regret. I'd overreacted.

I almost get whiplash at how quickly I looked at the door when someone knocked. I thought it was Reed.

"Hey."

Wyatt hovered in the doorway with a giant bear in his hands. I press my lips together as he extends the gift to me.

"Thank you."

I cast my fingers through the fur. He pulls a chair to my bedside and places his clasped hands beside my feet.

"Why didn't you tell me?"

His question was valid, but I don't know for certain. I don't know why I never told him I'd been sick. A part of me was afraid he'd judge me, or that he would treat me differently. It's what everyone at school did. I was no longer Olivia. Everyone saw me as *cancer girl.*

"I was afraid you'd look at me differently."

"I don't."

I wanted to believe him, but the clenched half-smile was a dead giveaway, a look I've become accustomed to. He reaches for my hand and intertwines his fingers in mine.

"This has been the best summer ever, and it's all because of you." He said. "I don't want to lose that. Or you."

My chest tightened at his confession. I folded my arms in on myself.

"You don't have to give me an answer right now." He said. "You have other stuff to deal with."

He leans over the bed to place a kiss on the corner of my lips. My eyes glanced at the door even after he'd left. I wasn't sure who I was hoping would walk back in.

Reed

The traumatic memories of last summer are like a *Jack-in-the-box*. It keeps getting winded up, only to reappear. It's as if my life is a horror movie and I'm forced to endure the same dreaded day for eternity.

I'm losing Olivia right after I got her. Just like last year.

I think back to that day a year ago, the conversation between her parents. The words they spoke cannot be repeated.

It would ruin everything.

I remember lurking around the corner eavesdropping on their heated discussion, only to be caught in the act. Her mother pleaded with me not to tell anyone. Especially Olivia.

There were multiple reasons I swore myself to secrecy. The main reason was that I loved them like my family, and I didn't want to sabotage anything. The Huxleys are good people, except Mr. Huxley. To me, he's the devil.

A week had passed since everything went down at Olivia's party, and she'd been free to go home after the doctors reassured her she'd only overexerted herself. I'd almost collapsed in relief when we received the news.

But she's been distant.

I'm at odds about what the right thing to do is. I just want to protect her. *All* of them.

"Earth to Reed." Connor said as he waved his hands in front of my face.

I stood frozen in the middle of the rink with the puck at my feet. Marcus looked at me with a raised brow.

"Where did you go?"

"Sorry," I said. "Got a lot on my mind."

Connor glides past me, stealing the puck.

"Girl trouble again?" He asked.

I nod my head and twirl my stick in my hand.

"Olivia has been avoiding me."

I must look like a kid who was told he couldn't have another slice of cake. It felt great not having to hide my feelings anymore, but it was also unusual.

"She just needs some time," Marcus said. "We all had a huge scare."

I nod knowing I'm just overthinking, but I can't help the hornets of insecurity stinging me. I needed to talk to her.

"As happy as I am for both of you," Connor said. "It's still weird that you're into my sister."

"I second that." Marcus said.

I chuckled at their antics before hitting my helmet to get my head back in the game. I take Connor by surprise as I skate behind him before gaining momentum and stealing the puck from him. The simple move ignited all our competitiveness.

Our bellows echoed throughout the arena as Connor stole the puck from Marcus and sent it flying with a powerful slapshot. We raised our hands in celebration, appreciating the skillful move.

We turn to the sound of clapping. Mr. Huxley is leaning against the entryway of the rink, acknowledging Connor's play.

"Good job, kid." He said. "You just need a bit more practice."

I bite my tongue, resisting the urge to tell him to *fuck off.* He's always been hard on them.

"What are you doing here, Dad?" Marcus asked.

He tucks his hands in his trouser pockets.

"I need to talk to you both." He said.

His gaze showed he wanted me to leave.

"Whatever you have to say, you can say in front of Reed." Marcus said.

Connor nods in agreement. We remove our helmets and skate to the benches, taking a seat around Mr. Huxley. He intertwined his fingers and shook his legs as we waited for him to tell us something. By the look on his face, disaster is about to strike.

"I got a call from Mr. Keller." He talked about our coach. "He's retiring, and he wants me to take over."

I hope that doesn't mean what I think it does.

"What did you say?" Marcus asked.

"I accepted the job."

Connor's brows furrow.

"That means we'll have to move."

Mr. Huxley bites his lip, avoiding Connor's burning stare. I can't blame him for being pissed off. Moving for your senior year isn't ideal.

"You can stay with your mother if you want to."

What?

"I'm not following." Connor said.

Mr. Huxley takes a deep inhale through his nostrils.

"Your mother and I are getting a divorce."

I keep my gaze on my skates, unable to look at their heartbroken reactions. A part of me expected this, but it's become real.

"What the *fuck*?"

Connor launches out of his seat, staring his dad down.

"Connor, please calm down."

I wince. That is the worst thing you could tell an angered person, *especially* Connor. He tosses his gloves to the ground before storming off. I look at a comatose Marcus. His dad reaches over to place his hand on his shoulder, but Marcus shoves him away before storming off in the same direction as Connor. My jaw clenches as the back of my neck burns.

"I told you not to fuck this up."

His eyes burn with frustration as if I caused all of this.

"Who do you think you're talking to?"

I tower over him with my arms folded across my chest.

418

"I'm talking to a douchebag of a father," I said. "This is going to destroy Olivia. We had a deal."

He stands up and looks into my eyes with a menacing glare.

"Tell her." He said. "She'll end up hating you for keeping it a secret."

I wanted to punch him in the mouth, but the truth wounded me. I drop my head, giving up the fight. He walked past me, bumping his shoulder into mine as he exited the stadium. I lower myself onto the bench and place my head in my hands.

Everything is falling apart, and I can't help but feel responsible. I raise my head at the sound of footsteps. Marcus hovers under the archway. He gazes at me with glossy eyes and red-blotchy cheeks. I don't know what I expected to hear from him, but his uttered words blew my mind.

"We cannot tell Olivia."

28

Olivia

Ever since I was released from the hospital, things haven't felt right. Life has been testing me, and it's as if it wants me to fail. I'd been so certain about my future with Reed until Wyatt confessed his feelings to me.

Should it matter?

Would it be idiotic of me to give up a potential relationship with Wyatt? Or would it be idiotic of me to give up everything I've reignited with Reed for something uncertain with Wyatt? Each relationship has a potential risk or reward. It's up to me to decide which risk is worth taking.

My love for Reed is like the stars on a cloudy night. It may sometimes be overshadowed, but it always shines under the surface. Or is our love like an outdated movie franchise, with a few sequels too many?

I've always had honesty with Wyatt. He'd always been upfront, whereas Reed always left me with doubt.

And secrets.

Today was the last day at the beach house and I'd busied myself with packing everything I wanted to take with me to college. I was halfway through my packing when I heard my mother yelling at Conor to get out of the pool. I rolled my eyes and continued with my work until Reed's euphonic voice called for Connor, sending me back into a spiral.

The summer has been a whirlwind. I never expected to meet Wyatt or to like him as much as I did. Yet, I never anticipated having to see Reed every day. Falling in love with him again was never part of the plan. The moment I saw him step out of his car on that first day of summer, I knew I was doomed. The only thing holding me back is the fear of the unknown.

I know I must decide and I'm running short on time. I reach for my phone and scroll to his name before exiting the chat and scrolling to the next name. My fingers hover over my screen as I read through previous conversations. I bite my lip, wondering if I'm making the right decision, but it's best to rip the Band-Aid off. I type out the text and give it a double-check before pressing send.

Hey, can you meet me at the beach in ten minutes? I have something I need to tell you.

The sea charges on the rocks below my feet, scattering the tiny pebbles. An icy breeze blows from the North, showering the banks with a salty mist. The small waves crash against the shoreline, sparkling as the sun's rays cast down to the admiral blue water. My dress sashays with the breeze as I dig my heels in the sand to speed up my stroll once I catch sight of the familiar figure retreating from the beach. The moment I reach him, I wrap my arms around his neck.

"Thank you for coming."

I pulled away to gaze into his pensive eyes.

"It sounded important."

I nod as I tuck a strand of hair behind my ear.

"I've been thinking a lot about your confession."

He stared into my eyes, as if he was trying to gauge my thoughts. His eyes narrowed to slits. I avoid his gaze as my eyes burn. My bottom lip quivers as my chest feels heavy. He knew I made my decision, and it wasn't him.

"It's always going to be him, isn't it?" Wyatt asked.

I avert my gaze and shift about, uncertain of how to let him know my reasoning.

"I never regretted meeting you. What I felt for you was so pure. You unlocked my heart when I thought I lost the key. Yet, my love for him is like the sun on a rainy day. It may not be visible, but it's always there."

He bit the inside of his cheek as he folded his arms across his chest.

"He's a lucky guy." He said. "I hope he knows it."

I tried not to let the guilt rule me. I cared more for Wyatt than I thought, this conversation clarified it. However, it could never compare to the complexity of my and Reed's relationship.

He leans down to place a kiss on my cheek before strutting off with a lowered head. I reach into my pocket for my phone to check the time. I hope I'm not too late.

I had sent the text to both, but my impulsivity kicked in, owing Wyatt an explanation after everything he's done for me, and I hope it hasn't cost me a chance to rehash things with Reed.

I ran as fast as I could in the sand, but the dampness from the waves made it feel like quicksand. I spot Reed in the distance, gazing at the sunset. The orange-gold stretched far and wide. The vibrant colors looked as if they were brushed upon an artist's canvas.

"I didn't think you'd still be here."

He looked at me over his shoulder as if trying to determine if I was real or a figment of his imagination. He turns back to the sun.

"I couldn't leave. My brain told me to go, but my heart held onto hope you'd come."

His words inflamed my heart. He waited for me. I'd been almost an hour late, but he'd still waited for me to show up. I tuck my dress underneath me and take a seat beside him, digging my toes into the sand.

"A part of me wants to erase every moment of last summer," I said. "To forget I ever loved you and have you back to just being my brother's best friend."

I sigh as the breeze whips through my locks.

"But a part of me knows that summer was the greatest time in my life," I said. "It was the reason I kept fighting."

He twists his body to face me. His eyes lock with mine, looking at me with such adoration that would put all the classics to shame.

"When you got sick, it forced me to imagine a future without you." He said. "I realized there isn't one without you."

He cupped my cheeks in his hands.

"I'd given up on my dreams when I thought I'd lost you." He said. "I never thought we'd get this far, but I know if I were to let myself dream for a moment. My future has one constant, and it's you."

He leans down until our foreheads meet, looking into my eyes as they radiate with warmth.

"You were always my certainty, Olivia Huxley."

His eyes sparkle with deep affection, as if our entire love story is flashing through his mind like a movie montage. As if he was reliving every kiss, every touch, every declaration of our love. His eyes were my reassurance. All the doubts I had diminished like a raindrop in the ocean. He was worth the risk. Reed will forever be a part of my life, and despite all the hardships, he will forever be my soulmate.

Our love is like a phoenix. It burns until it fades to ashes. Only to rise again, stronger and wiser.

Author's Note

DO YOU HAVE A LOT OF
UNANSWERED QUESTIONS?

FEAR NOT! There is upcoming
works.

Books 2 and 3 in the series will follow
Olivia's college journey. Book 4 will
take us back in time to where Reed
and Olivia's romance first sparked.

ALSO... A book will be dedicated to
Connor's story.

Printed in Great Britain
by Amazon

41998758R00245